My Soul Sings

Sequel to *Sweet Sanctuary*

My Soul Sings

Kim Vogel Sawyer

A NOVEL

Wings of Hope

EST. 2013

Published by Wings of Hope Publishing Group
Established 2013
www.wingsofhopepublishing.com
Find us on Facebook: Search "Wings of Hope Publishing"

Printed in the United States of America

Sawyer, Kim Vogel
My Soul Sings/Kim Vogel Sawyer
Wings of Hope Publishing Group
ISBN-13: 978-1-944309-14-5
ISBN-10: 1-944309-14-4

This is a work of fiction. Names, characters, incidents, and dialogues are products of the author's imagination and are not to be construed as real. Any resemblance to actual events or people, living or dead, is entirely coincidental.

Cover artwork by Kim Vogel Sawyer.
Typesetting by Vogel Design in Hillsboro, Kansas.

For Tamela Hancock Murray,
agent extraordinaire,
who never lost faith in what could be.

The Lord is my strength and my shield;
my heart trusted in him, and I am helped:
therefore my heart greatly rejoiceth;
and with my song will I praise him.
Psalm 28:7 (KJV)

1

"Hey, buddy, need some help?"

The gruff voice startled Jeremiah from his drowsing. The bus had come to a stop. He jerked his bleary gaze to the dirty window. The scene outside the window was not the Polish countryside, and for a moment panic struck. Where was he? He squinted, focusing on a small, wood-slatted building. The sign on its front read Shyler's Point Post Office. His racing pulse returned to normal. Ah, yes... Arkansas. All was well.

With a muffled grunt, he swung his feet to the aisle. The vibration from the rumbling engine tickled the backs of his legs as he sat sideways on the cracked vinyl seat. He locked the knee positions of his leg braces, then pushed himself upright. Keeping a grip on the back of the seat, he finally answered the grizzled driver.

"Yes. Thanks for asking. Could you hand me my crutch and my bag, please?"

The driver popped the gear shift into Park and waddled to Jeremiah. He grunted as he retrieved the items from under the seat. The man handed Jeremiah the crutch, but he kept hold of the bag. "I'll git this for ya. You just go ahead." He stepped into the space between seats to allow Jeremiah to pass.

Jeremiah sensed the driver's presence behind him as he made his way through the narrow aisle to the bus steps. The hair on the back of his neck prickled, and he reminded himself that the driver meant no harm. Clutching the handrail firmly with his right hand, he balanced himself with the crutch under his left arm and bounced slowly down the two steps to the dusty street. He turned and took the bag.

The driver grinned, tipping his grimy fedora. "There ya go, buddy. Enjoy your time in Shyler's Point, y'hear?"

Jeremiah nodded. "Thanks. 'Bye, now."

The roar of the engine drowned out the last two words as the driver pumped the gas. The bus growled out of sight around a sharp bend in the road, leaving Jeremiah standing in front of the tiny Post Office with the smell of gasoline filling his nostrils. He glanced up and down the street. As he had been warned, Shyler's Point wasn't much of a town. Only five or six buildings sat haphazardly around a central grassy area that must be the town's park.

And there wasn't a soul around. The stillness sent an eerie shiver down his spine, and he instinctively scanned the area for soldiers. He shook his head, forcing the fear away. He was no longer in Europe. No soldiers resided in Shyler's Point.

Lord, grant me Your peace.

The prayer helped, but where were his brother's friends? They were supposed to meet the bus. He glanced at his pocket watch. Just after seven thirty. Now he understood. The bus had been ahead of schedule. He looked around again, taking in the lengthy shadows falling to the east. It appeared later, perhaps because the mountains blocked the sun's rays as it dropped toward the western horizon. Well, there was enough light for him to walk to their house.

According to the directions he'd received in his letter from Holden Winters, who was the town's doctor as well as his brother's good friend, the Winters' home rested on a knoll behind the general merchandise store. He turned a slow circle, seeking the building in question, and a sound drifted across the park, settling in his chest and filling him with a feeling of home.

"*...So I'll cherish the old rugged cross, 'til my trophies at last I lay down...*"

The tune rang out in four-part harmony, but no instrument seemed to underscore the voices. Keeping a firm grip on the handle of his travel bag, he began hitching in that direction, drawn by the familiar old hymn. Dust stirred as he dragged his heavy shoes across a winding dirt path. Behind a large brick building with a second-story balcony, he located a small clapboard church with a belled steeple.

"...*Then He'll call me some day to my home far away, Where His glory forever I'll share...*"

The song seemed to call to him as he made his way past a half-dozen tired-looking vehicles and twice that number of wagons with mules attached clustered in a disorganized manner beneath towering oak and maple trees. He crossed a sloping expanse of thick grass and patches of blue Johnny jump-ups—a familiar sight from his childhood—to the church's front porch. Six treads climbed upward. He'd never make it with his bag in hand.

He dropped the bag on the grass. Who would bother a bag left on a church's doorstep? Slowly, he clumped up to the landing and paused outside the open double doors to catch his breath. The music rolled through his chest, making him eager to be a part of what was happening inside the building. An enclosed entry perhaps six feet deep separated the porch from the sanctuary. Squaring his shoulders, Jeremiah scuffed across the plank floor and stepped into the small sanctuary. Backless benches formed two rows. He glanced around for a place to sit, and the final words to the hymn filled his ears. He joined in with his deep baritone, unable to remain silent.

"I will cling to the old rugged cross, and exchange it some day for a crown."

The tall, dark-haired man behind the simple wood podium at the front seemed to spot Jeremiah. A smile broke across his face—a face that seemed familiar although Jeremiah had never met him before. At the smile, people began turning in their seats to look over their shoulders. A hush fell over the room, and Jeremiah found himself under the scrutiny of perhaps fifty townspeople.

One little tow-headed boy on the right turned clear backwards, kneeling on the seat and pointing at Jeremiah's braces. "Hey, Ma, you figure that guy got hurt in the war?"

Jeremiah winced. Undeniably he had been hurt in the war, which was part of the reason he'd agreed to come to Shyler's Point—to try and recover—but it wasn't war that had created the problem with his legs. He'd found a way to reconcile himself with the pain in his legs. Would the pain in his heart prove to be as conquerable?

"Be quiet, Jimmy!" The mother scolded in a loud whisper, tugging him back around. But the child kept his head cranked, openly staring at the braces that supported Jeremiah's weak legs. The child wasn't the only one staring, but Jeremiah kept his gaze aimed forward, trying to ignore the curious looks.

The man left his spot and walked briskly to Jeremiah. In the silence that followed the mother's admonition, his footsteps echoed hollowly, sending a shiver of apprehension down Jeremiah's spine. How he disliked the thud of falling footsteps… The man extended his hand, the smile still splitting his face. "Jeremiah Hatcher, welcome to Shyler's Point!"

Everyone sat straight up, and whispers of recognition swept across the small crowd.

Jeremiah shook the dark-haired man's hand, and realization struck. This must be Micah's friend, Holden Winters. Micah had indicated they looked enough alike to be brothers. With Holden's sturdy build, dark hair, and piercing blue eyes, he could easily pass for a Hatcher boy.

"Holden?" Jeremiah queried, just to be sure.

"That's right." Holden's smile swept the room. "Folks, this is the reverend I told you about—Reverend Jeremiah Hatcher. Let's make him welcome."

Calls of greeting broke out across the room, accompanied by the patter of applause. A petite, auburn-haired young woman with the rounded belly of advanced pregnancy bounded down the aisle and captured Jeremiah's hand.

"Jeremiah, it's so good to meet you! I'm Callie, Holden's wife." Her face pinched with an apology. "But you're early—we weren't expecting the bus until eight. You must have thought we forgot about you."

"No—not at all. I knew I was early." Jeremiah squirmed, aware of their watching audience and the number of gazes that seemed pinned to his leg braces. Obviously Holden and Callie hadn't warned the congregation about his handicap. "I heard the singin', and I just made myself at home."

"I'm glad you did." Holden gestured to an empty spot at the end of one bench. "Will you join us? Wednesday is usually Bible study night, but tonight we're having a gospel-sing since our preacher is out of commission and can't lead a preaching service."

A wrinkle-faced woman sitting on the aisle tapped Holden's elbow. "But this feller's gonna do the honors next week, right, Doc?" Her hat that resembled an upside-down soup kettle decorated with wilted sunflowers.

Holden nodded. "That's right, Flossie. Reverend Hatcher will deliver our sermons until Reverend McCleary is back on his feet." He turned to Jeremiah. "But for now, Jeremiah, have a seat and make yourself at home."

Jeremiah started toward the closest bench at the back, but Callie slid her hand through the bend of his elbow. She guided him to the front bench where she seated herself and smiled up at him.

He leaned his crutch against the bench next to Callie's hip. All sets of eyes seemed to bore into him. Having spent the last several months trying to stay out of sight, it was disconcerting to be the center of attention. Perspiration broke out over his body. He bent over to pop loose the locks at his knees, and the gentle click seemed like a rifle shot. Once the locks were released, he sat quickly, catching himself with his palms to keep from tumbling backward off the bench. Several gasps exploded behind him, followed by sighs of relief, and he gritted his teeth.

Callie touched his arm, and he glanced in her direction. Her smile put him at ease. Looking into her sparkling green eyes, he understood why his brother had been so taken by her. But God had different plans for Micah, and Micah was now seeing those through. When would God reveal His plan for Jeremiah?

Holden had returned to his position behind the podium. "Who else has a song they'd like to sing?"

A rustle of movement indicated eagerness. From the corner of his eye, Jeremiah spotted a delicate, swan-like movement. Intrigued, he leaned forward slightly. A slender young woman wearing a simple blue-checked dress held her hand timidly in the air. Her honey-colored hair, blunt cut at shoulder length, swung forward and hid her profile from view. For reasons he couldn't begin to comprehend, in that moment it became very important for this girl to be chosen.

Jeremiah jerked his gaze to Holden. Had he spotted the hesitant gesture? To his relief, Holden was smiling the girl's direction.

"Yes, Tessy, what song would you like to sing?"

Tessy, Jeremiah's heart repeated. *Tessy*.

A sweet, reedy voice came from behind the veil of

hair. "'The Church in the Wildwood,' please, Doc."

Someone behind Jeremiah tittered. "Reckon she oughtta know about wildwood places, huh? Practically lives in the woods like a wild thing." Other giggles followed the comment.

The girl apparently heard, too, because she dropped her hand to her lap and bowed her head. Jeremiah's temper flared. But Holden spoke, pulling attention away from the rude whisperers.

"That's a wonderful choice." Holden raised his arms and started, "There's a church in the valley by the wildwood; no lovelier place in the dale..."

Jeremiah sang, but he kept his gaze angled toward the young woman. As the song took wing, she slowly straightened, face lifting toward the front once more. His heart thumped in gratification. She raised her slender hand and pushed the satiny strands of hair behind her ear, revealing a fine-boned profile. Jeremiah's throat caught. She was beautiful—as dainty and fine-featured as a China doll.

Then her chin turned slightly and she caught him staring. Her eyes widened and her cheeks splashed pink. For a moment her lips faltered, the song fading, and Jeremiah wondered if he should look away to keep from causing her discomfiture. Yet he found himself nearly mesmerized as her expression relaxed into a smile, and she tipped her head to stare unabashedly into his face.

The singing seemed to fade into the background as Jeremiah and the lovely young woman focused solely on each another. The bright, healthy glow in her cheeks was such a contrast from the young women he had encountered in the past years. His heart beat high in his chest as her large, unusual gray eyes remained fixed to his. A myriad of emotions washed over him like waves bouncing against the shore. Admiration for her beauty. Compassion for the unkind words she'd no doubt overheard. Appreciation for her attention.

Deep appreciation for her attention.

Because not once did her gaze drift to the silver braces that had so captured the interest of those seated behind him. For the first time, Jeremiah felt as if a woman was seeing him as a man rather than a cripple.

Tessy McCleary could scarce believe that the handsome preacher man who'd come from overseas was looking at her with approval in his eyes. Such beautiful eyes, too. Deep blue like the sky in late afternoon when a storm was brewing, or like the delphinium when it first opened its bud. When she'd heard his voice join in on the last song and had peeked over her shoulder, she'd thought she was seeing an apparition. Surely no man could be that handsome. But then Doc Winters had spoken to him, and he'd spoken back, and everybody stared, so he had to be real.

And now he was looking at her like…like she mattered.

Well, wouldn't take him long to see her like everybody else did. All the folks around here knew she wasn't good for anything more than traipsing. They were right, too. Made her heart heavy to know how this man would surely soon turn away from her. But he wasn't turning away now. He wasn't now.

She forced her lips to form the words to her hymn, finishing it with the congregation, her gaze still locked with the preacher man's. "…No place is as dear to my childhood as the little brown church in the vale."

Doc Winters called on Betsy Travers and another song started, but Tessy didn't sing. Neither did the preacher man, Jeremiah. He just kept looking. His thick hair, cropped short and rather mussed, as if slept on, was the color of walnut husks fully dry—a deep, earthy brown with a sheen. He had a dimple in his left cheek—showed when the corners of his lips tipped up in a shy smile, like they were doing now. His dark brows were full and they arched over his eyes rather than hooding them the way some other men's did. She liked that. Gave him an open, honest appearance. His pale chin was peppered with a full-day's whisker growth, but she could see it was square and strong—a determined chin. Probably had to be determined to march down a center aisle with a bunch of folks gawking like they'd never seen a stranger.

Tessy swallowed. Now here she sat, gaping just like they had. Her cheeks blazed hot. She should look away. But she couldn't do it. What was it about him that drew her like a hummingbird to a forsythia bush? If Pete could see her now, he'd have something to say. She'd lost her senses the moment she'd heard Jeremiah Hatcher's voice raised in song.

Had he bewitched her? Her grandmother had talked of such things. Pop never preached it from the pulpit, so it had to be foolery. Like the tales the old folks told about hauntings and bad luck signs. All foolery, she tried to convince herself even as her heart pounded in fear of its reality. The way she felt pulled to him, though... If it wasn't bewitchment, what was it?

Stop gawking—look away. It was hard, but she turned her face to the front. Relief washed over her. If she could do it, she wasn't bewitched. All that talk was foolery, just as she'd thought. Her face still forward, she peeked by turning her eyes in his direction. Her heart thudded wildly in her chest. The preacher man—Jeremiah— hadn't turned his face.

He was still looking.

And it left her feeling light and airy inside. She lifted her chin, pressed her shoulders back, and opened her mouth to join in the song. A smile hovered in her heart. She knew without even looking. The preacher man was watching.

2

At eight o'clock, Holden offered a closing prayer. Many of the townspeople came by Jeremiah's bench, shook his hand, and welcomed him to Shyler's Point. Callie's aunts, Vivian and Viola, were especially kind. Jeremiah smiled and thanked each person, but he found it difficult to stay focused. His gaze wanted to follow the alluring young woman from the opposite end of the bench. She had slipped out the moment the "Amen" was uttered, leaving him feeling strangely alone.

When the last townsperson moved down the aisle, Jeremiah snapped his leg braces into position, then followed Holden and Callie outside. To Jeremiah's delight, the young woman who had so captured his attention stood in the corner of the porch, her gaze heavenward.

Callie smiled. "Hello, Tessy."

Tessy gave a start. She brought her gaze to Callie. "Hi, Callie. Doc Winters." Her gaze swept past Holden to light upon Jeremiah. Only then did a small smile crease her face. "Preacher." Her voice was breathy, as if she feared being heard.

"Would you like us to walk you home, Tessy?" Holden took Callie's arm and guided her down the steps.

Tessy gave a quick, eager nod, her hands clasped together at her waist. "Yes, please."

Jeremiah moved awkwardly one step at a time, leading with his crutch and holding tight to the rickety railing. He stepped aside and Tessy bounded down the steps on bare feet, her toenails broken and rimmed with dirt. Apparently she saw where his gaze went, because she covered her left foot with her right and curled her toes under.

"Felt so good to have the grass tickle my soles, I left my shoes on the stoop at home." She peered at him through a fringe of thick eyelashes, her chin low.

Jeremiah offered a smile. "I imagine it's a pleasure, running your bare feet through the grass. I don't blame you for taking advantage of the opportunity."

Her answering smile warmed him all the way to his own toes which were protected by sturdy black lace-up shoes. Up close she truly was exquisite—fine featured and delicate, with a light spattering of freckles across her nose. She would make a beautiful ballerina, so graceful were her simple movements as she fell into step beside him.

Holden picked up Jeremiah's bag and set off across the grass at a leisurely pace. "I should introduce you two. Jeremiah, this is Tessy McCleary, our preacher's daughter."

Jeremiah assumed the daughter of a preacher would have more confidence. And clean feet. Yet despite Tessy's natural grace and beauty, she gave the distinct impression of self-consciousness as well as earthiness. "Well, then, we'll probably get to know each another quite well." He wouldn't mind it, either. "I'll be spending time with your father as I prepare for my sermons."

"I don't stay to home durin' the day." Her gaze skittered in his direction, then darted away, as if afraid of meeting his eyes.

"Oh?" Jeremiah slowed his steps when the path sloped downward. "Do you have a job that takes you away?"

"No." But she didn't elaborate, and he wasn't sure where to take the conversation from there.

Holden stopped in front of a rustic log house. "Here you are, Tessy. Have a good night."

Tessy gave a brisk nod and bounded up the dirt walkway. She bent down to snatch up a pair of brown oxfords resting on the end of the warped top step of a narrow stoop, then disappeared behind the door without a backward glance.

Oddly, Jeremiah felt deflated by her sudden departure. He stood, looking at the house which appeared to be two square cabins joined by an enclosed breezeway also constructed of logs. There was no porch, only the two-step stoop, but along the entire front of the house, blooming flowers brightened the drab exterior of worn logs. "What a unique-looking dwelling."

"It's a dogtrot."

Jeremiah turned a frown on Callie. "Excuse me?"

She grinned and pointed to the cabin. "The construction—it's called a dogtrot. Two rooms connected by a hallway, or 'dogtrot.' The earliest settlers found it the best way to make a larger living area and still use the forest for their building materials."

Jeremiah examined the house. Yes, he could see the sense of Callie's explanation. The length of the tree trunk would determine the size of the room. By connecting two cabins, the builder could double the size of his home.

"I lived in a dogtrot in the mountains before I came to live with my aunts," she went on. "This particular dogtrot is the oldest in Shyler's Point, built by Azariah Spencer, one of the first two men to settle this area. He owned the first business in town, too—a fur trading post which gradually developed into our general store. His grandson, Andrew, now runs it."

Jeremiah gave Callie a teasing smirk as he began shuffling forward, his crutch sinking into the dirt walkway. "You make a great tour guide, Mrs. Winters."

She laughed. "It's fun to have someone new to share

things with. Most everybody in Shyler's Point already knows all there is to know about it. But please call me Callie. We don't stand much on formality here in the mountains."

"Callie it is." The woman's easy acceptance of him raised a feeling of belonging. He allowed his gaze to take in the sights as they moved slowly toward the Winters' home. Houses—some constructed of logs and others of clapboard—sat far apart with winding paths leading from one to another. A few windows sported a blue-starred banner indicating a family member served in the armed forces. Only one of the homes had a yellow star. As he passed it, he offered a brief prayer for the family of the young man or woman who had been killed in the line of duty. The banners made him sad, and he turned his focus to the landscape.

Though the surroundings were very different from his childhood home of Arlington, Texas, Jeremiah appreciated the simple beauty of this little community perched within the majestic Boston Mountains. Dusk brought an unusual reverence to the landscape. Gentle moonlight tipped the trees. An owl's querying hoot sounded in the distance, while crickets chirped in unison beneath flowering bushes. Sweet scents drifting on a mild breeze tantalized the senses. He'd only been in Shyler's Point an hour, and already he understood why Holden and Callie chose to make this their home. The natural beauty seemed to settle itself within his soul.

He breathed deeply, attempting to absorb the scents and sights and sounds, using it as a balm for the wound he carried in his heart. So much horror he'd witnessed while in Europe. So much anger, pain, and ugliness. *Lord, thank You for bringing me to this place of peace and beauty. Already my heart feels calmed, my thirst for loveliness being quenched. Thank You...*

"Well, here we are." Once again Callie's voice interrupted his private thoughts.

Holden opened the narrow gate to the picket fence guarding their small yard, and Jeremiah struggled over the rock threshold. Large, flat stones with moss growing in between formed a pathway. In the gloaming, he had some difficulty placing his crutch to avoid the cracks between the stones. He breathed a sigh when he reached the porch and its solid wood steps.

Callie skipped ahead of him and opened the front door. She poked a button near the doorjamb and light spilled through the doorway, illuminating the porch floor.

Jeremiah followed the path of light into the house. He glanced around, warmed by the simple furnishings. "This is very homey."

"Thank you." Callie beamed her ready smile. "I moved in with my aunts right after my seventh birthday, so I pretty much grew up in this house. It hasn't changed much in all these years, but it's comfortable."

"All these years." Jeremiah grinned. "Makes you sound like an old lady."

Callie laughed. "That sounds like something Micah would say."

Holden nodded, smiling at Jeremiah. "I'm glad that ornery brother of yours managed to arrange this for us. The whole community is pleased to have someone willing and able to fill in for Reverend McCleary. Going without church services for six to eight weeks wasn't an acceptable option for anyone, yet no one felt qualified to step into the pulpit."

Jeremiah shrugged to mask a yawn. "I'm glad it worked out, too. The timing was perfect, with my return correlating with your need. Micah told me Reverend McCleary had some sort of emergency surgery?"

"His appendix ruptured. He's very lucky to be alive."

"Did you do the surgery?" Jeremiah knew that Holden had a small clinic in one room of his home, but he couldn't imagine him performing emergency surgery in his simple setting.

"I operated, Callie assisted." Holden linked fingers with Callie. "And several people prayed. He survived."

Jeremiah shook his head in wonder. "I'm impressed, Dr. Winters."

"Don't be. God's the real healer. I do my best and leave the rest up to Him."

"I like your attitude, and I believe I'll borrow it when I step behind the pulpit of the little chapel on the knoll." These days Jeremiah felt sorely unqualified to preach.

"We're glad you're here," Callie said.

"And I'm happy to be here, despite the sad reason that brought me. I already find myself feeling very much at home in your mountains. It's so peaceful."

Callie and Holden exchanged an odd look. He said, "Let's show Jeremiah his room."

The pair led Jeremiah up a short hallway, Callie's cheerful chatter accompanying them. "You'll be staying in Aunt Viola's room, so please excuse the feminine bric-a-brac."

Jeremiah's heels dragged as tiredness took over. "I hope I haven't put her out."

"Oh, no. Aunt Viola moved in with Aunt Vivian several months ago, when Aunt Vivian's husband became ill. Then, when he passed away, Aunt Vi chose to stay with Aunt Viv rather than coming back here." Callie switched on the lamp which stood on a small, scarred stand next to the iron bed. "They've lived together most of their lives, so they're perfectly happy to be together again."

Holden put Jeremiah's bag on the end of the quilt-covered bed. "Callie put paper and pens in the desk drawer, and there's a chamber pot in the lamp stand's cabinet. Is there anything else you need?"

Had they provided a chamber pot so he wouldn't have

to stumble around in the dark seeking the outhouse? "Are you this obliging with all of your guests?"

Callie's sweet laugh rang. "You're not just a guest. You're like family already since we love Micah so much, and you are very much like him. I hope you'll be at home with us."

Jeremiah inwardly berated himself for the less than gracious question. He opened the bag and began removing his clothes. "You're both very kind. I appreciate your hospitality."

Callie moved to the door, her movements surprisingly graceful in spite of the ungainly bulk she carried up front. "I know you're tired, so we'll let you get settled. If you want something to eat before you turn in, the kitchen is down the hallway and to the left. Help yourself to anything you want in the ice box. The milk is fresh, and there are cold cuts if you feel like making a sandwich."

Jeremiah liked being treated like a member of the family rather than catered to like a guest. "I appreciate it, but I'm too tired to eat. I'll be asleep soon, I'm sure." His right hip ached, and unconsciously he rubbed the joint.

Holden's gaze drifted to his hip, and sympathy creased his brow. "Our mountain pathways will be difficult for you."

It was more a statement than a question, but Jeremiah answered anyway. "Up and down is always harder than straight across, but I'll manage."

Approval shone in Holden's eyes. "Micah said you were a fighter. He's really proud of your accomplishments. Especially in Europe."

Jeremiah raised his eyebrows. "He told you?"

Callie's forehead furrowed. "Was he not supposed to? You're almost all he talks about in his letters to us. He was so pleased that Justina's adoption would be official soon, now that he and Lydia are married. We were amazed when he told us how the little girl came to be with him."

Less than three weeks ago Jeremiah had stood beside his brother and witnessed the joy in Micah's eyes as Micah recited the vows binding him to Lydia. Micah's only regret had been Callie and Holden's absence. Callie couldn't travel so far at this stage in her pregnancy.

She covered her lips with her fingertips. "Have we breached a confidence?"

Jeremiah hadn't realized Micah told anyone outside of the family about Jeremiah sneaking the little Polish Jewess into America, but he wasn't surprised given their close friendship. "No, you haven't breached a confidence. But..." He paused, searching for the best way to word his request. "I would appreciate it if you wouldn't tell the people of Shyler's Point what I did in Europe. There is still so much anti-Semitism... Some people might not understand." He wouldn't admit his overwhelming guilt, which he longed to set aside.

Callie touched Jeremiah's sleeve. "The community

knows you were in Europe, but all they know is that you worked for a Russian church. Micah told us there could be trouble if the wrong people found out how the crew of the Red Cross ship transported Jewish children. The townspeople don't know the rest, and there's no reason for us to share it, unless you want to later on."

Jeremiah doubted the day would ever come. He wanted to forget his involvement in trying to help the Jewish people escape Hitler's rampage. He had so miserably failed at the task. "Thank you."

Holden slipped his arm around his wife's waist. "I thought we were going to let Jeremiah turn in." He touched Callie's cheek and smiled down at her.

Callie shrugged. "I thought so, too, but you know me—chatter, chatter, chatter!"

Holden sent a wink in Jeremiah's direction. "Better get used to this chatterbox. Callie could talk the hind legs off a mule."

She laughed and lightly bopped her husband's chest. "Ignore him, Jeremiah. He says that to everyone, but not once have we seen any mules wandering around with only front legs, so I hardly think it's the truth."

Jeremiah enjoyed the teasing repartee the couple shared. Callie and Holden possessed the type of relationship he would like to find with a young woman. Now that Micah was married, Jeremiah was the only one of the five Hatcher brothers who hadn't settled down to start his own family. His aching hips reminded him that marriage and family might be an impossibility for him. What woman would marry a cripple?

Tessy McCleary appeared in his memory. Gratitude swelled as he remembered how her gaze never wavered from his face. Her fragile beauty had left an impact on him, and there was something else about her. Something he couldn't pinpoint, but something that intrigued him. He frowned.

Holden cleared his throat. "Enough talking for tonight. Jeremiah will be here at least a month so we'll have plenty of time for conversation." Holden escorted Callie into the hallway. "Jeremiah, we'll see you in the morning. Sleep well." He closed the door, and their whispers and muffled laughter faded as the pair moved away.

Loneliness descended. He sighed and leaned his crutch against the wall between the bed and the stand housing the chamber pot. He pulled aside the lace curtain that shrouded the open window above the lamp stand. The beautiful Boston Mountains stood tall and majestic behind the house, the woods shadowed as dusk fell.

I will lift up mine eyes unto the hills, from whence cometh my help...

The words drifted through his mind, and he smiled. "Yes, Lord, I believe this view is going to be a wonderful help for my bruised heart. Thank You for bringing me here."

He watched the mountain disappear into shadows, then he sank down on the edge of the mattress and unstrapped the buckles on his braces with slow motions. He placed them on a straight-backed chair standing near the bed. Rolling onto the mattress, he slipped off his pants and unbuttoned his shirt, then he lay on top of the quilt. The room was warm—no need for covers. He reached over and snapped the switch on the lamp, sealing himself in darkness. Electricity, but no indoor bathroom. Electricity was a treat, something he'd never had in Poland.

He raised his fists and pressed them against his closed eyelids. He needed to stop thinking about Poland. But Callie's comment about Micah being proud of what he'd accomplished in Europe played through his memory, bringing a rush of remembrances. But he'd done so little over there. Not enough. Never enough. Would God forgive him for not doing more?

Tears stung as the images of helpless children being herded away beside their frantic parents flooded his mind. The confused, frightened cries and the sound of many feet pounding along the pavement filled his ears as effectively as if it were really happening. He pressed his knuckles against his eye sockets until bright light appeared behind his lids and the pain took precedence over the memories.

Deliberately he tuned his ears to the gentle sounds outside the open window. The breeze whispered down the mountain, lifting the stiff lace curtain until it swished gently along the sill. Locusts sang, and a bullfrog's low croak silenced them for seconds at a time before they resumed their chorus. His stiff frame began to relax.

He drew upon the images he'd encountered in this small mountain community—the towering maples, the rustic homes, the church's small but proud steeple, the sweet-smelling flowers dotting yards and lining pathways, the welcoming smiles of the people…and Tessy's unusual gray eyes as they met his gaze without once drifting to his braces.

Jeremiah, eyes closed, smiled. Only the memory of Tessy now remained. With the image of the young mountain woman's face firmly in his mind, he let his arms flop outward. Such a gift she'd given him when she looked at him and not his braces. Tomorrow he would find her, thank her, and let her know how much it meant to him to be truly seen.

3

Tessy checked to make sure her lamp had enough oil to keep it burning all night. If the lamp went out before daybreak, she'd awaken with night terrors. She pushed the oil lamp to the center of the table beside her bed where she wouldn't accidentally bump it if she rolled over in her sleep. Once the lamp was secure, she lay back against plump feather pillows and stared at the shadows dancing on the floral-papered ceiling.

The erratic movements caused her heart to pick up its tempo, and she whispered, "Just the curtains blowin'. Nothin' spooky about that. No reason for fear." Gradually her pulse slowed to a normal rhythm, and she sighed in thankfulness.

She turned to her side, curling her fists beneath her chin. That new preacher—Jeremiah Hatcher—had fixed his blue-eyed gaze on her during the singing. She smiled, the remembrance sending tingles down her spine. Such a fetching man. Why'd he looked so hard at her? Maybe because he could see the ill wind surrounding her. A preacher would be able to discern such things as that.

Tessy shivered despite the warmth of the room. She closed her eyes for a moment, deliberately conjuring the image of his face, of his tender expression. If he'd been fearful of her, she would've known it. She'd seen fear often enough in the faces of the people in town. The preacher had looked, but his looking hadn't been the watchful kind. He seemed to find pleasure in sharing a smile with her. The tingle came back to her spine, ending in a shiver. Was she cold? She flipped the patchwork quilt across her bare legs.

Walking along beside Jeremiah Hatcher on the way home from the church, listening to the noise of his feet dragging on the pathway, Tessy had felt at ease. Most times new folks put her on edge. But not this new preacher man. What was it that made him different? Maybe it was his hindrance. Those braces and crutch slowed him down. Did they help him look at things differently since he wasn't able to rush here and there? She flopped to her back. And maybe she was being silly, lying here mooning over a man because he'd smiled in her direction.

The town thought differently, but Tessy was like most young women. She longed for love and family and a home to call her own. The preacher's kindness had stirred those longings in her breast.

She sighed, turning her attention once more to the flitting shadows that danced above her. Might as well set aside those thoughts. A preacher would want somebody smart, somebody who would be a help in his ministry. Tessy would be more of a hindrance than those silver braces on his legs could ever be. She'd be tripping him up all the time. He'd said he would be spending lots of time with her father. So she'd better make sure to be away when he came. Looking into Jeremiah Hatcher's eyes gave her ideas she had no right to consider.

Sadness washed over her. She wished things were different—that she was different. But she was an ill wind. Always had been, always would be. Not even Pop being a minister had changed that. And already she liked this preacher too much to want pain to come to him. She sensed a sorrow under the surface. She wouldn't add to it. The preacher would surely arrive mid-morning, not before. She'd get up early and head out. Maybe visit Ol' Gordy.

A weight pressed into her chest. Hurt to think of staying away from him. But it was for the best. Tessy would rather be hurt herself than bring pain to the man who had looked at her with such kindness. She couldn't give him reason to change that look to one of fear and disapproval.

The sun was shooting fingers of light over the treetops when Tessy set off into the woods the next morning. Her backpack contained a light lunch of bread and cheese, a burlap-wrapped jar of water, and her drawing pad and pencils. She'd hike to Ol' Gordy's valley and spend the day with him before coming home in time for supper. Surely she'd miss Jeremiah Hatcher's visit by staying gone that long. People were safer when she was away. The protectiveness she felt for someone she'd only met was new, and she savored it. She'd do what it took to keep him safe—even if keeping her distance was hard.

She raised her gaze, squinting as beams broke through cottony clouds and lit the morning sky of cornflower blue. The sky reminded her of Pop's reading from the Bible about when Jesus would return to earth. She liked to look at those shining beams and imagine Jesus, in a flowing white robe with his arms outstretched, standing right amidst the clouds, beckoning all of His children to draw nigh.

Pausing in her walk to fully absorb the sight, she tipped her head to the side and pondered whether she'd get to go, too, when Jesus called His own to Himself Tessy hoped He would recognize her heart. She'd given it over to Him when she was a wee girl—had even been baptized by Pop in the creek behind the church—but sometimes she worried that she wasn't good enough to get into Heaven. She sure hoped Jesus wouldn't leave her behind.

Wasn't much on this earth that she needed to stay around for...

She headed on, her feet moving silently over mossy ground layered with decaying leaves from years of seasons changing. A striped green lizard darted from beneath a rock, fixed his beady-eyed gaze on her, then skittered back into hiding. Tessy laughed and crouched down. "Now, now, little fellow. I won't bring you no harm." But the lizard didn't come out, so she lifted her gaze.

The brilliant red leaves of Indian Paintbrush growing nearby caught her eye. Tessy smiled, shaking a finger at the showy plant. "You can't fool me with your colors. I know that's not a blossom you're sportin'. But you sure are pretty. Figure I'll just add you to my book."

She sat cross-legged on the ground and draped her skirt over her knees. She removed her pad and colored pencils from her pack. In only a few minutes she had recreated the cluster of corollas within brightly-colored bracts. She added a bit of the stem and a few green leaves, then held the pad at arm's length. Scowling, she picked up the red pencil to darken the shady areas at the base of the upper leaves. She looked again. "Better." Smiling in satisfaction, she replaced the paper and pencils in her pack and stood. Giving a wave, she called, "Good-bye, pretty leaves. Keep growin'!"

Tessy knew if the townsfolk heard her talking to animals and plants it would only serve to further their belief that she was "tetched" in the head. But she didn't care. Animals and plants didn't turn away like people did. She figured God spent as much time creating the things of nature as He had creating the people. Why shouldn't they be given some attention, too?

A bit farther along, she stopped again to sketch pale blue Eyebright blossoms that grew bravely within a patch of rough ground. It took longer to produce the delicate, four-petaled blossoms with their intricate stripes. With painstaking care, she drew the multiple strands of buds and flowers, even adding the coarse backdrop of crumbling sandstone. Time slipped by while Tessy drew, fully engrossed in her sketch. When she finally raised her head, she was startled by the shortened shadows. The sun was well into the sky. Even the morning clouds had drifted away, leaving only a few wisps of white.

If she didn't hurry, she wouldn't reach Ol' Gordy's place today. She took a drink from the jar, then repacked her bag and set off once more, her footsteps sure as she crossed the rougher terrain leading to the hermit's home. Although she continued to enjoy the beauty of nature around her, she didn't stop again until she looked down into the valley where the cabin was hidden. As always, the valley was shrouded in gray, too deep and overgrown to receive the sun's cheerful rays. She'd never understand why Ol' Gordy chose to live in such a gloomy place when the mountains were so full of glory elsewhere.

She'd asked him a long time ago why he lived in the valley, and his answer left her baffled.

"They that dwell in the land o' the shadder o' death, upon them hath the light shined."

She must have looked as confused as she felt, because he had smiled gently—such an incongruous expression in his pock-marked, dirty, whisker-shrouded face—and said softly, *"My valley's dark like death, but I know where to find the light if'n I want to."*

It didn't make sense, but quite often Ol' Gordy didn't make sense. Tessy liked him anyway. He wasn't afraid to be with her. He treated her kindly, talked to her like she mattered to him. Kind of like the preacher had.

"Now, you wasn't going to think about Jeremiah Hatcher." She shook her head to clear the thought, then cupped her hands beside her mouth and hollered, "Ol' Gordy! You home? It's me, Tessy!"

Her voice bounced against the granite back wall of the valley, repeating itself in a hollow echo. She waited, and in a few moments Ol' Gordy appeared in the doorway of his ramshackle cabin. He looked upward, his bulbous nose raised like a bloodhound seeking its quarry, then he lifted his bony arm and waved.

"C'mon down, Missy. Tea's on."

She smiled in response to his gravelly invitation and bounded down the mountainside as quickly as possible with her pack bouncing against her spine. When she stood beside him, he grinned and shook his head.

"It be so long 'tween visits, thought you'd fergot all about me."

Tessy laughed and wiped the sweat from her forehead with her fingers. "Not likely, Ol' Gordy. Just been explorin' on the mountaintops. Enjoyin' how things are blossoming up there."

Ol' Gordy's beady brown eyes lit up. "Got new pictures to share?"

Tessy nodded. She enjoyed sharing her drawings with Ol' Gordy. He was the only one who'd been allowed the privilege of peeking at her artwork. She trusted him not to make sport of her penchant for putting things that pleased her senses on paper.

"Come in then. Water's hot fer the sassafras leaves, an' the lamp's burnin'. We'll sit an' sip, an' I'll take me a gander at yore colored drawin's."

Tessy followed Ol' Gordy into the murky depths of his cabin which had been built over the opening of a small cave. The tiny room always smelled musty and damp, but the companionship she enjoyed with Ol' Gordy was worth having her nostrils assailed by the pungent odor.

Ol' Gordy pointed to the rough hewn table and waved a calloused, arthritis-bent hand. "Sit yerself down. I'll fix ya that tea, then we kin chat."

Tessy took out her sketchpad and pulled the oil lamp

closer while he crushed sassafras leaves into two chunky mugs then doused them with boiling water. He wheezed as he crossed to the table and plunked the mugs onto the dusty table top. Breathing in this damp air must be hard on his lungs, but she knew he'd never move out.

"There now." He lowered his bony frame onto the three-legged stool across from Tessy. "Best let that sit fer a bit. Mighty hot."

"Thanks." Tessy turned her sketchpad toward him. She watched Ol' Gordy's eyebrows raise in approval as he examined the pages. Felt good to have his admiration. His kindness warmed her even more than the sassafras tea.

"Well, now, Missy, they's all purty, but I gotta tell ya I like the one o' the Purple Saxifrage best."

Tessy laughed. "But you've seen that one already. It's not new."

He chortled, too—a gruff, rolling sound like pebbles shaken in a bag. "Oh, I know, I know. But how you put them pink an' purple colors together so's you kin see each little blossom on the spike an' drawed the rock clefts shieldin' 'em in… Why, Missy, I kin almost smell 'em, they're so real. You got a real knack, thet you do."

Tessy basked in his praise, her chest expanding with pleasure. "Thank you."

The old man leaned his elbow on the table, his gaze faraway and dreamy. "Yep, a real knack… My mama, she was handy with makin' purty things, too. Only she di'n't use paper an' pencil. She was a hand with fabrics an' threads. Embroid'ry, it's called. Flowers, 'n honeybees, 'n woodland critters like the tiny chipmunk or sassy jaybird. Took up a needle an' those threads an' made them things come to life on a bit o' muslin." He shook his head, darkness creeping into his eyes. His musing tone turned bitter. "'Til her fingers was so scarred from workin' that she cou'n't hold a needle no more. She'd sit an' cradle her embroid'ry hoop 'gainst her chest, an' the tears'd roll down her cheeks, but she never made a sound. Mournin'... Her soul was mournin'..."

Tessy got the feeling that Ol' Gordy had slipped away somewhere—somewhere unpleasant. She touched his arm, and he jumped, swinging his gaze back to her. "You miss her, don't you?"

He sat upright and removed the sheen of tears from his eyes with a vicious swipe of his wrist. He gave a careless shrug, but the whiskers on his chin quivered. "She's been gone long enough that I've got used to it. Ain't so bad no more."

Tessy didn't believe him. She suspected Ol' Gordy was just as lonesome as she, isolated as he was in this deep valley away from everyone and everything. "I packed some bread and cheese. Want to go sit on the creek bank and have a picnic?"

HIs face lit, the sadness gone. "I'll pick some mint

leaves fer chewin'. That'll perk up the taste buds."

Tessy gave a smiling nod. "That'd be perfect." She was eager to go back out. Despite the deep shadows, the sun hovered somewhere above the mountaintops. The damp gloom of Ol' Gordy's cabin was fast becoming cloying. She scooped up her pack and moved outside with with the old man huffing on her heels. She released a sigh of relief to be in the fresh air. "Come on, Ol' Gordy. You choose the spot."

She allowed him to lead the way. The dismal feeling from being in the cabin washed away with the creek's cheerful chatter and the breeze whispering between the mountains. She handed a chunk of cheese to Ol' Gordy. What was Mama serving for lunch? Had the preacher stayed to eat with Mama and Pop? Try as she might to put aside the thought, her stubborn mind kept envisioning Jeremiah Hatcher seated at her table, smiling and talking to Mama, while Tessy's chair sat empty.

4

The hour-long conversation Jeremiah enjoyed with Pastor McCleary apparently wore the older man out. While the reverend snored in the opposite side of the dogtrot cabin, Jeremiah sat at a square table in an uncomfortable bentwood chair, and Mrs. McCleary clanked things around on the stove. The fragrant aromas of onion soup and fresh bread filled his nostrils. He swallowed the saliva that pooled in his mouth.

"It's just a simple meal," Mrs. McCleary said as she ladled soup into his bowl, "but soup's something that keeps on the stove and is ready whenever somebody's hungry."

Jeremiah smiled. "I hope that wasn't an apology. It smells wonderful. I can imagine how welcome that smell must be when someone comes through the door." He looked toward the door, hoping Tessy might come in, drawn by the inviting scent.

Mrs. McCleary plunked the pot back on the stove,

then crossed to the table to sit down across from Jeremiah. "You want to say the grace, Preacher?"

Jeremiah brought his gaze to the woman across the table. He blinked, disappointed. "Won't your daughter be joining us?"

"No, I don't expect her."

"Oh." Jeremiah cleared his throat. "She made other plans?"

Mrs. McCleary sighed. "Tessy's off in the woods. Her pack's gone, as well as half a loaf of my fresh-baked bread. I don't imagine I'll be seeing her 'til late this afternoon."

Jeremiah's heart fell, but he plastered a smile on his face and folded his hands. "Well, then, I'll pray and we can eat." He bowed his head and offered a brief word of thanks for the meal. At his, "Amen," Mrs. McCleary repeated the word, and they picked up their spoons.

Jeremiah blew on the soup before carrying it to his mouth. He swallowed and raised his eyebrows. "Mm. This tastes as good as it smells."

Mrs. McCleary beamed. "Why, thank you, Preacher. I suppose it's the fresh ingredients that come right out of my own garden." She sipped the broth from her spoon.

They ate in silence for a few moments before Jeremiah remembered the cutting comment made in church the night of the singing. "Does Tessy go into the woods often?"

Mrs. McCleary lifted a napkin to dab her mouth.

"Tessy is very good at traipsing." She frowned, her gaze on her soup bowl. "Seems it's the only thing she's good at." Then she raised her face and her eyes widened as if surprised by her own words. "I don't mean to say she's a good-for-nothing. Tessy's a big help to me—especially since her father has been sick to his bed. It's just that Tessy is…different…from her brother."

"Oh?" Jeremiah took another bite, careful to keep too much interest from creeping into his tone. He didn't want to frighten the woman into silence. "How is that?"

"Our Pete is a college professor. Went to the University of Arkansas in Fayetteville and got his degree in mathematical sciences." There was no denying the pride shining in Mrs. McCleary's eyes as she spoke of her son. She enunciated each syllable. "Now he's teaching at Harding College at Searcy. Our Pete's a very intelligent man, and he gets along so well with people. Most everyone likes Pete."

Jeremiah felt the stirrings of dislike for the man, and he hadn't even met him. "So if Tessy is different than Pete, are you saying she isn't necessarily intelligent and doesn't get along well with people?"

The older woman blanched. "Well, when you just say it out like that, it sounds much worse." She put down her spoon and placed her hands in her lap for a moment, her troubled gaze settling on Jeremiah. "You see, Preacher, Tessy and the folks in town… Well, they just never learned to know each another, I suppose. Tessy had a rough time coming into the world, and maybe I protected her a bit too much in the beginning, held her away from people. And…they just grew on without her. Now she's a grown woman—turned twenty-two last April—and she doesn't really belong."

Jeremiah set aside his spoon and gave Mrs. McCleary his full attention. "Mrs. McCleary, may I have your permission for something?"

"For what?"

Jeremiah interlocked his fingers and rested his wrists on the edge of the table. "I'd like to spend time with your daughter. To be her friend. Perhaps, if I'm able to befriend her, the town might begin to look at her differently."

Mrs. McCleary pursed her lips. "Well, Preacher, I don't have a problem with you trying. But you have to realize that you're talking about trying to overcome a whole lifetime of feelings. Not easy to do."

"God never promised that things would be easy. Only that He'd give us the strength to carry on."

She nodded, her face thoughtful. "I imagine you'd know quite a lot about that, seeing as how you rely on help every day just to walk."

Jeremiah offered a sad smile. Mrs. McCleary referred to the physical act of walking, but her words brought to mind his spiritual walk. He had certainly leaned heavily on the Lord to survive the past difficult years. Now that those years were over, he felt as if he was stumbling more than at any other time in his life, trying to find his pathway. Mrs. McCleary looked at him expectantly, her head tipped, as she waited for his response. He said, "You're right, Mrs. McCleary. You might say I've learned that I can do all things through Christ who gives me strength."

"That's a good lesson, Preacher."

He sighed. "Yes, it is. 'All things' should include convincing the town to open its arms and accept Tessy, shouldn't it?" He smiled and picked up his spoon once more. "This is delicious. I know it's onion soup, but there's something else in the broth. Are you willing to share your recipe with me?"

The woman's face brightened with pleasure. "Why, Preacher, you cook?"

They enjoyed a lighthearted conversation about Jeremiah's limited kitchen skills as they ate. When they finished eating, Jeremiah returned to the minister's room for an afternoon of study and talk. They invited him to stay for supper, but instead he set out for town.

He moved slowly past the post office, pausing a few minutes to visit with a pair of older men in striped overalls who sat under the porch eave and whittled. Curled shavings from cedar sticks dropped in slow motion onto the porch floor, the pungent scent pleasant. With a wave he moved on, hitching toward the looming general store owned by the grandson of one of the first settlers to Shyler's Point. Jeremiah smiled to himself, remembering

Callie's little history lesson. Her pride in Shyler's Point was obvious, and Jeremiah experienced a prickle of envy. Callie was so certain where home was meant to be. He wished he had that same certainty.

Using his crutch to balance himself, he stepped up the single step that led to the wide, wood-planked porch fronting Spencer's General Merchandise. Twin screen doors protected the store from insects. Jeremiah opened the right one, sending a cowbell into raucous clamor. He stepped into the spacious store. The whir of a rotating fan set on top of a Frigidaire behind the counter provided a pleasing breeze. A variety of odors—sour pickles, sweet apples, and tobacco—tickled his nostrils.

A plainly dressed young woman with her red hair pulled into a tight ponytail traded a small brown bag for a coin from a shirtless, barefoot boy. When the child turned, Jeremiah recognized him as the boy who had been hushed in church. The boy's gaze lit on Jeremiah's braces, then traveled upward until he met Jeremiah's gaze.

Jeremiah smiled. "Hello. You're Jimmy, right?"

The boy nodded. He appeared to be eight or nine years old, with white blonde hair that stuck up in a cowlick at his forehead. Several copper-colored freckles scattered randomly across his cheeks. "How'd you know?"

Jeremiah shrugged, assuming a serious air. "Ministers are pretty smart. They're supposed to know everything, aren't they?"

Jimmy shook his head. "Can't know ever'thing. Only God knows ever'thing."

Jeremiah nodded, keeping his face solemn. "You're right. I stand corrected."

Jimmy pointed at Jeremiah's braces with a grimy finger. "How come you use those things? Sure are shiny."

The woman gasped, and she turned her back.

Jeremiah glanced down at himself, pretending to examine the braces. "You mean my braces?"

Jimmy nodded eagerly. "That's what you call'em? Braces?"

The woman seemed to lean her ear in his direction, listening in.

"Yes, they're called braces." Jeremiah swallowed a chortle at the woman's eavesdropping. "I use them because if I didn't, I would fall down. My leg muscles aren't as strong as yours. The braces help my leg muscles hold me up."

"How come?"

"I had a sickness when I was very young—called polio. It damaged the muscles in my legs."

Jimmy nodded gravely, his eyes grew wide. "You'd really fall down?"

Jeremiah was touched that the child seemed concerned rather than amused. He had encountered other attitudes in his lifetime. "I would."

"I fall down sometimes, see?" The boy deposited his

bag on the counter, then leaned over to tug the patched leg of his overalls high above his right knee. A healing scab came into view. "Did that fallin' down the hill behind my house. Hurt like fury."

Jeremiah examined the knee with all due attention. "Mm-hm, I imagine it did." Then he snapped his finger and straightened, pretending to get a good idea. "I think I have a cure for that ill. Would a grape Nehi make your leg feel better?"

Jimmy dropped the pant leg and bounced to Jeremiah's side, licking his lips. "A grape Nehi?"

"Yes. I was going to have one myself. I'd gladly treat you, too."

The boy bounded to a cooler in the corner and grunted against the weight of the lid. A steamy mist rose from the depths of the large white box. Jimmy stood on tiptoe and reached inside, and bottles clanked. He removed one bottle and waved it in the air. "Here's a strawberry, Preacher! Want that?"

Jeremiah clumped closer, his crutch echoing against the wood floor. "No, I'd like grape. Can you find a grape for me?"

"Sure!" The boy went in again, this time retrieving a bottle of grape Nehi. "Here ya go!"

"Thank you, Jimmy." Jeremiah took the bottle. "Now get one for yourself."

Once more Jimmy turned his attention to the cooler,

and as he reached, the cowbell clanged. The child lifted his head to look toward the door. His mouth formed an O, and he leaped away from the cooler. The lid slammed with a resounding *bang*! He pressed his back against the cooler, his eyes wide and fearful.

Puzzled, Jeremiah looked toward the door, but he saw no cause for alarm. Tessy McCleary, her dress rumpled and hair disheveled, stepped over the threshold and stopped. Jimmy scuttled toward the screen doors, keeping a wide berth around Tessy.

"Jimmy, you forgot your candy!" the woman behind the counter called, but the boy scuttled out the door without responding. The screen door bounced in its frame behind him. The woman shrugged, plunking the little bag under the counter somewhere. "I s'pose he'll be back."

The child's reaction didn't seem to surprise Tessy. She stood with her unsmiling gaze locked on Jeremiah.

The clerk swished a cloth over the counter. "What you need, Tessy McCleary?"

Her brusque tone made the hair on the back of Jeremiah's neck prickle. He took a slow step closer to Tessy. "I was offering young Jimmy there a soda, but he left before he could accept. Would…would you like a Nehi?"

Tessy's tongue sneaked out to swipe her upper lip. Clearly she was hot and thirsty.

He raised his bottle. Beads of condensation dripped

from his fingers onto the floor. "What's your favorite? I like grape best."

A shy grin twitched on her cheek. "I like strawberry."

Jeremiah beamed. "Okay, then. Strawberry for you." He put his bottle on the counter, ignored the scowl of the woman who stood with crossed arms, and moved to the cooler. He heaved the lid open and grinned at Tessy.

She sidestepped close enough to remove a bottle of strawberry Nehi. She swept the moist bottle across her forehead, releasing a light sigh. She offered another small smile. "Thanks, Preacher."

He wanted to tell her to call him Jeremiah, but not with their audience frowning from behind the counter. "You're welcome." He lowered the lid, then he crossed to the counter and dug in his pocket for change to pay for the sodas.

The woman took his money without a word. She pointed to the end of the counter. No smile touched her face. "Opener's over there. Help yourself."

Jeremiah hooked the cap of his bottle against the metal opener and popped it loose. The cap bounced across the floor with a series of soft tings. He leaned his hips against the counter and lifted the bottle to his mouth to enjoy a long swig. "Ahhh…"

Timidly, Tessy stepped forward. But when the cap on her bottle came loose, soda fizzed up and spewed out. She thrust the bottle away from her body and strawberry

Nehi dribbled down Jeremiah's pant leg, leaving a pink stain on the tan twill, then puddled on the floor. Horror broke across Tessy's features.

The woman dashed around the counter. "Consarn you, Tessy McCleary, look what you done! You did that on purpose!"

Jeremiah held up his hand. "Miss McCleary must have grabbed the bottle that Jimmy picked up. I saw him shake one."

The woman swung on Jeremiah. "All the bottles in the cooler an' she lights on the very one ready to spray all over the place? Tell me that wasn't on purpose!"

Tessy hung her head. "I'm so sorry." She plunked the bottle on the counter and raced from the store, leaving the cowbell clanging angrily in her wake.

"Good riddance." The clerk dropped to her knees and began scrubbing with the floor with a rag. "Wish she wouldn't come in here if all she's gonna do is cause trouble."

Jeremiah bit his tongue to hold back an argument. He boiled with indignation and at the same time his heart ached for Tessy's humiliation. Of all the luck, to choose the one bottle that had been upset by careless handling. What would the clerk have done if he had spilled the soda? Would she have used that accusing tone on him?

From the floor, the woman glanced up. "You best go get them pants rinsed out, Preacher, or that stain'll set for good."

Jeremiah looked again at his pant leg. She was right. He started to take another drink, but the soda had lost its appeal. He placed the bottle on the counter next to Tessy's and turned toward the door. His heart felt heavier than his feet as he shuffled out onto the porch. He stood for a moment, his gaze turned in the direction of Tessy's home. Her mother's words played through his memory—*"Tessy and the folks in town... Well, they just never learned to know each another, I suppose."*

There was much more involved here than a case of not knowing each another. There seemed to be real animosity toward Tessy. Even fear, in the case of young Jimmy. Having witnessed the rejection firsthand, he was determined to find a way to mend the broken bridge between Tessy and the community. To do that, he needed to discover the root of the problem.

He clumped down the steps and headed for the Winters' home. He knew where to find answers. From his own personal Shyler's Point tour guide, Mrs. Callie Winters.

5

Jeremiah stayed quiet during supper, pondering why Jimmy ran in fear the moment Tessy entered the store. The storekeeper's rudeness was habit. Otherwise would she have behaved so badly in front of a minister? And Tessy herself had seemed to accept the discourteous treatment without question.

When the dishes had been washed and put away, Callie turned to Jeremiah with an inviting smile. "Holden and I like to sit on the porch in the evening and watch for the first star. It's cooler out there. Would you like to join us?"

Jeremiah nodded, eager to finally ask the questions plaguing him. Callie and Holden shared the swing hanging from sturdy chains, and Jeremiah chose a wicker rocker nearby. Holden stretched his arm along the back of the swing and tugged Callie securely against his side. She snuggled, grinning up at her husband, and he bestowed a light kiss on her forehead.

Watching, Jeremiah experienced a niggle of envy. Would he ever have the pleasure of a wife and family? It would take a special person to accept him with his limitations as well as have the willingness to serve as a minister's wife. Did such a woman exist? He sighed.

"You've been rather distracted this evening, Jeremiah." Holden's voice cut through his thoughts. "Did your meeting with Reverend McCleary not go well?"

Jeremiah shook his head. "I had a good visit with him. I assured him I would keep his normal routine for services as closely as possible so people would feel comfortable with me behind the pulpit. He shared a few passages that he's used for sermons recently so I wouldn't repeat something that's been covered, and he gave me the go-ahead to preach as I feel led." He paused, furrowing his brow as he recalled his lunch conversation with Mrs. McCleary. "No, my meeting with the reverend went fine…"

Callie rested her head on Holden's shoulder, concern in her eyes. "But something's bothering you. Are you missing your family?"

Jeremiah chuckled. "Callie, I've been away from home for several years. Although my family is never far from my thoughts, I'm not homesick, if that's what you're asking." Then he sobered. "But there is something bothering me. Maybe you could help make sense of it." Briefly he shared his experience in the general store. "It all seemed so odd—the way the child was afraid, and the anger in place even before Tessy spilled that strawberry Nehi. Yet Tessy acted as if nothing unusual was happening. What has she done to deserve such ill treatment?"

Callie and Holden exchanged a glance, then Callie sat up straight and sent Jeremiah a serious look. "Jeremiah, there's no easy way to say this, so I'm just going to say it straight out. Folks around here say Tessy is a jinx."

Whatever Jeremiah had expected, that wasn't it. He blinked twice then shook his head to clear it. "Did you say Tessy is a *jinx*?"

Callie grimaced. "I know it sounds outlandish, but unfortunately it's true. For as long as I can remember, the people of Shyler's Point have looked on Tessy as someone who carries bad luck."

Jeremiah wished he could laugh, convince himself Callie was playing a joke, but her expression was too serious. "You really mean it, don't you?"

"I'm afraid she does." Holden set the swing into motion. "I noticed what you described when I first came here, and it bothered me, too. But how to fix it?"

"Shouldn't that question have been asked years ago?" Indignation built in Jeremiah's chest. How could the community be so cruel? And how could people like Callie and Holden—obviously good, Godly people—allow it to continue?

Callie sighed. "I understand your frustration, but it

isn't as easy as you think to change the town's attitude. Many of the hill people believe strongly in superstition. The ideas have passed down through the generations." She gave a gentle shrug. "My family never put much stock in it, probably because my grandparents were such devout Christians, but it's hard to persuade someone to throw out a belief firmly pressed upon him by his beloved great-great-grandmother."

Holden said, "Actually, many of the superstitions are simply common sense, such as never walk under a ladder. The hill people might argue that a leaning ladder creates a triangle when compared to the wall and ground, and to walk beneath it disrupts the trinity of Father, Son, Holy Spirit, which will bring a curse upon you. But the common sense of the thing is that the paint bucket hanging at the top of the ladder could fall and give you a nasty bump on the head!" He and Callie both laughed.

Jeremiah held out his hands. "But, Holden, this isn't a matter of avoiding walking a certain pathway. This involves the intentional mistreatment of an innocent person." Hitler's intentional mistreatment of the Jews rose up to taunt him. "The superstitious idea of a jinx… And to choose the daughter of the town's preacher! Why would they do that? And why haven't Tessy's parents protested it?"

"They have protested it, although I don't think strongly enough." Sympathy glowed in Callie's green eyes. "They are really very mild-mannered people."

"Mild-mannered or not, to allow an entire community to mistreat your child over some ridiculous superstitious nonsense..." Jeremiah's heart constricted.

Callie sighed. "I'm sure it's hard for you to understand. Frankly, I don't understand a lot of it, myself. But in the eyes of the people living here, there are sound reasons to believe that Tessy is a jinx."

"*Sound reasons?*" Jeremiah gaped at Callie. "How can you put the words *sound reasons* and *jinx* in the same sentence? The idea of a jinx is very unsound."

Callie shifted closer to Holden. "Let me see if I can explain. I was very young when Tessy was born, so I only know what my aunts have chosen to share with me, which isn't much because, like you, they think it's all nonsense. But from what I've been able to pick up here and there, Tessy had the misfortune of being born on Friday, the thirteenth of April. According to stories told, a lone crow walked back and forth along the clothes line while Anna was in labor until the baby gave her first cry, then the crow cawed and flew away."

"And that means...?"

Callie released a sad chuckle. "One crow is supposed to mean bad luck. Couple that with the whole Friday the thirteenth superstition, and Tessy was doomed from the beginning."

Jeremiah raised one eyebrow. "You don't really believe that."

Holden snorted. "Of course, we don't. But the point is, many in town do." He crossed his leg and bounced his foot. "My personal feeling is their own nervousness around Tessy has produced what they refer to as an 'ill wind.' Whenever she's near, they expect something bad to happen, so they inadvertently drop things, spill things, trip over things... It isn't Tessy's fault, really, but they assume she's the one to blame."

Jeremiah folded his arms over his chest. "Ridiculous."

Holden nodded. "Very. But how to change it? One thing I've learned while I've been here—I can try to take care of their physical needs, but only if it doesn't interfere with their home remedies. Those superstitions are firmly imbedded."

Jeremiah rolled his eyes. "I still think it's ridiculous."

Callie glanced at Holden with a wry smile before turning back to Jeremiah. "Ridiculous or not, there's been a lot of fuel for that fire over the years. Now, keep in mind I don't blame Tessy—it's simply circumstance—but it does seem that misfortune follows her. I remember once she came out of the general store, and a horse bolted, raced down the middle of the street, and nearly trampled two older ladies. Of course, logically, her sudden appearance probably frightened the horse, but the townspeople read more into it than that. You see, they day before, one of those ladies had scolded Tessy for picking flowers out of her garden. The townspeople thought Tessy scared the horse on purpose to get even with the lady."

Jeremiah frowned. "Tessy seems so timid and tender-hearted—she wouldn't seek revenge."

Callie nodded. "You don't have to convince me. Convince them." She waved a hand in the direction of the town. "That's just one example. I could tell you more."

"I don't want to hear more." Jeremiah sighed. If he were a superstitious person, perhaps he would read more into the spewing soda pop. "Tessy's mother said she and the town have never really learned to know each another. What has kept Tessy separate from the town?"

"I'm not sure exactly what Mrs. McCleary meant, but Tessy was a sickly child. She missed more days of school than she attended. Then, in the summer of '30 or '31—I can't remember which for sure—we had a typhoid epidemic. It was a terrible time. Several people died, including Tessy's grandmother, and both Tessy and her mother were sick. When it was over, Tessy didn't come back to school. Her parents said she was still weak, but months went by, and we'd see her out wandering in from the woods when we walked home from school in the afternoons. That told us she had recovered, but she didn't come back. After awhile, we stopped worrying about it. Tessy and school just didn't go together well, I guess."

"Didn't go together well…" Jeremiah considered Tessy's timid demeanor, her difficulty in meeting one's gaze. An unwelcome thought intruded. "Do you think she has some sort of…problem…that keeps her from learning?"

Callie wrinkled her nose. "I don't think she's dimwitted, if that's what you mean, but she might feel that way compared to her brother. Peter McCleary is one of the smartest people I've ever met." She laughed lightly, flipping her hands outward. "Of course, compared to Pete, most of us would feel dull. He truly is brilliant."

Jeremiah chuckled, too, although the topic left him uneasy. "This Pete must be a lot like my oldest brother, Joel. That boy had more smarts than the rest of us put together, and Mama always said there were no dim bulbs amongst her offspring. Still, teachers expected Jonah and Amos, who came after Joel, to be as smart as he was. It was hard on them, living in Joel's shadow."

He gave a one-shouldered shrug. "Of course, the teachers were pretty well 'broken in' by the time Micah came along, so there were no unrealistic expectations placed on him, and as for me…" He forced a laugh, a cover for the hurt that pressed in his chest with the memory. "Teachers usually took one look at my braces and decided I was just as crippled in my mind as I was in my legs. They didn't expect much at all. Which was good, because then no matter what I did, it was considered brilliant."

He emphasized his Texas twang as he continued the story. "Took advantage of that a time or two 'til my mama got wind of it. She had a way of inspirin' one to do his best in all circumstances." He rubbed a hand up and down on one of his back pockets to emphasize the words.

Callie and Holden both burst out laughing. Callie said, "You know, from what you and Micah have said, your mother must be one terrific lady."

Jeremiah wouldn't argue. "Mama is somethin'. If it wasn't for her, I probably wouldn't be up and walking. After my illness, my legs were so weak, an' it hurt to use them. I'd whimper and lift my arms to anybody who walked by, just beggin' to be carried. Of course, my older brothers, bein' protective, wanted to make me happy, so they'd scoop me up an' cart me along. One day Mama lined them all up next to me, where I sat like a toad in the grass, and said real sternly, 'No more of this totin'. God gave your brother legs, an' he's got to learn to use 'em. So the next one of you who picks him up is gonna be in hot water.' Must've seemed cruel, because they told Mama that it wouldn't be fair to leave me behind, it wasn't my fault that my legs had give out. But she said, 'If he wants to be with you badly enough, he'll find a way to get there.'"

He shook his head, smiling in remembrance. "I remember howling for all I was worth as my brothers trotted down the road without me. An' they looked back at me, real sorrowful, but not a one of them would dare to cross Mama when she'd lowered an edict like that one. So they started coaxin'. An' it took me a couple days, but when I finally figured out that they really weren't goin' to carry me, I started usin' my legs. An' now I can get most places on sunny days. Mama taught us boys a good lesson."

Holden nodded, his expression thoughtful. "That's a good lesson to all of us. God equips us for what He intends for us to do, and He provides encouragement, but it's up to us to follow through and actually walk the pathway He's chosen." He took Callie's hand, giving it a squeeze. "And aren't we all so much happier when we're following His footsteps?"

Jeremiah looked aside as the couple exchanged a warm smile. Although Callie and Holden had been married nearly four years, they still behaved like newlyweds, reminding him of Micah and Lydia. The prickle of jealousy stirred deep within his heart again. Would he ever find the kind of love these two couples shared?

Tessy appeared in his memory—her honey-colored hair sweeping across her cheek, her gray eyes turned attentively toward him, her sweet lips tipped into a hint of a smile. She was a pretty young woman even if she seemed haunted by something inside. What did she see when she looked at him, Jeremiah, the man—or Jeremiah, the cripple? He wanted to believe it was the former. He appreciated that she hadn't seemed impatient with his slower pace when they'd walked from church the other evening. She hadn't seemed focused on the shiny braces that kept him upright. She looked into his eyes—if her gaze was aimed in his direction. Often her gaze was aimed downward, but he was convinced now that wasn't a way of avoiding his braces, it was a way of avoiding her own insecurities. His heart ached for her to see herself as a person of beauty and worth. How could he reach her and convince her that she was a person of value?

The only thing he could think of was to change the opinion of the townspeople. If they stopped treating her as if she carried bad luck, then she would stop looking at herself in that way. According to Callie and Holden, however, the task might prove to be impossible. Then, as clearly as if she were seated beside him, he heard his mother's voice chide.

"For with God nothing shall be impossible."'

She quoted the verse from Luke any time he felt discouraged about the weakness in his legs, and she had turned out to be right. Jeremiah had gone on to do things the doctors had deemed impossible.

Nothing is impossible for You, Lord, he prayed silently as the swing chains creaked and a lone cricket made itself known beneath the slatted porch floor. *I'm trusting You to help me find a way to rid this town of their misguided beliefs. I'm placing Tessy in Your hands.*

"Jeremiah?" Callie intruded into his private thoughts.

"Yes?"

Silently, Callie pointed to the gate at the end of the pathway leading to the house.

Jeremiah looked, and his heart skipped a beat. He smiled. "Hello, Miss McCleary."

6

"Evening, Doc Winters, Callie…" Tessy swallowed, suddenly shy. "Preacher."

The doc and his wife stayed seated, but Jeremiah Hatcher leaned over and clicked something on his legs, then struggled to his feet. He smiled, and the tenderness she'd seen in his eyes earlier that day was there again. Set her heart into flutters. As if by its own volition, her hand rose to rest against the bodice of her dress.

"Good evening to you, Tessy." The doc pushed the porch swing into motion with his feet. The gentle squawk of the chains reached where she stood. "What brings you over? I hope no one is feeling poorly. Is your father all right?"

"Pop's restin' easy after havin' a good supper." Tessy curled her hands over the gate's pointed pickets. "Seems to be doing just fine."

"That's good to hear. Tell your mama I'll be by tomorrow morning to check on him."

"Thank you." A nervous giggle escaped. "I, um, come by to talk to…Preacher."

Even though the preacher stood under the porch roof in shadow, Tessy was sure his face brightened. A funny tickle climbed her spine. He made his way to the edge of the porch, his crutch leading with his right foot, the left foot following. "Yes, Miss McCleary? What can I do for you?"

His mellow tone, so friendly and kind, sent warmth from Tessy's scalp to her bare toes. She tightened her hands on the gate. "It's—it's about today, when I spilled that strawberry soda…"

Preacher shook his head, and she stopped. Was he hushing her? He made his way down the three porch steps and across the paving stones to the opposite side of the picket gate. When he got close, she saw no animosity in his eyes, only the tenderness she'd seen before. She bit down on the insides of her cheeks to keep from breaking out in a smile.

"I don't blame you at all for what happened in the store." He spoke softly, keeping his words between the two of them. "Before you got there, a little boy had taken out a bottle of strawberry soda and shook it around. He was excited. He wasn't trying to be mean. And then he put it back because I wanted grape. You just had the misfortune of latching onto the same bottle Jimmy shook. It wasn't your fault."

The word *misfortune* boomed louder than any other. She dropped her gaze, the word echoing through her mind. Misfortune always seemed to follow her. "Well, my fault or not, I feel bad that your pants got stained. I'd feel a lot better if I could set things right."

The preacher cleared his throat. "Miss McCleary?"

She didn't look up, afraid to see what might be lurking in his eyes.

"Tessy?"

At her given name, her chin shot up, and her gaze collided with his. Only kindness showed in his blue eyes. The relief she felt at his lack of anger was immense. "Yes, Preacher?"

"Two things." He held up two fingers, smiling gently. "First of all, there is nothin' to set right because you didn't do anything wrong. It was an accident."

His softly worded message washed over Tessy like a sweet oil, enveloping her in a healing warmth.

"Second, I really would like for you to call me Jeremiah rather than Preacher." He grinned, a single dimple appearing in his left cheek. "Except, o' course, when we're at church. Would you do that?"

Her heart pounded so hard she was sure he could hear it. She spoke his name, allowing the syllables to roll from her tongue. "Jeremiah..." She liked the way it felt.

"It's a beautiful name."

"Why thank you." He gave a teasing bow that made giggles build in her belly, but she held them back. "I happen to think you have a beautiful name, as well. Would it be all right if I used it instead of Miss McCleary? I have to admit, Tessy is a lot easier to say."

Tessy loved the way her name sounded when it came from Jeremiah's lips. He had a gentle way of speaking, of drawing the words out slowly as if savoring them. "I—I'd be pleased to have you call me Tessy." Her own voice sounded wispy and short of air. She pressed her hands against her stomach. "But, Preacher, I—"

"Ahem!"

Her face heated. "Jeremiah…"

His smile encouraged her.

"I'd like to fix those pants for you. Tomorrow's wash day, so it wouldn't be no bother to scrub 'em up with my family's laundry." She wanted so badly to right the wrong, no matter if he blamed her or not. She blamed herself. "Will you let me?"

Jeremiah's forehead puckered. Tessy could tell he was arguing with himself, trying to decide what was best to do. He didn't blame her for what had happened. It made her all the more determined to do something good for him in return for the favor of his kindness.

Finally he nodded. "All right, Tessy, if you insist on washin' these pants, I'll bring them by in the morning.

But"—he lifted a warning finger—"not because I think you're to blame. I'm doin' it because washing clothes is one of my least favorite tasks."

His eyes twinkled. He was teasing with her! The giggle that had threatened earlier erupted, and to her delight Jeremiah matched it with a deep chortle of his own. Felt good to laugh. And when the giggle died, a smile remained. She felt it tug clear across her face, and she did nothing to squelch it.

"Thank you, Jeremiah. I…I'll see you in the morning, then." She backed off a step, her gaze still locked with his.

"In the morning." He seemed as pleased as she at the prospect.

She raised a hand, reluctant to leave but aware that there was no good reason to keep standing by the gate. "'Bye, now, Jeremiah."

"'Bye, Tessy."

She hurried away, the warmth of the shared laughter still filling her chest. *I like him, God,* she admitted as she resisted the urge to look back and see if he still remained at the gate watching her. *He's such a nice man.* She frowned, her steps slowing as her thoughts added, *Please don't let nothing hurt him.* She knew God would understand what she really meant was, *Don't let me hurt him.*

"Good morning!"

The greeting brought Tessy's gaze up from the depths of the washtub, and her heart immediately jumped into double beats at the sight of Jeremiah Hatcher and Doc Winters stepping into the backyard. Doc waved a hand of greeting and headed into the house without pausing to chat, but Jeremiah came to stand on the other side of the washtub. He held a folded wad of damp tan fabric in his free hand. He looked very comfortable with himself in a pair of loose-fitting blue pants, a blue and white plaid shirt, and his familiar black shoes and silver braces. Tessy liked the way the blue in his clothing brought out the blue of his eyes.

Mama straightened, too, wiping the sweat from her forehead and beaming a welcoming smile. Mama looked as pleased to see Jeremiah as Tessy felt.

"Well, good morning, Preacher," Mama said. "You're just in time."

"That's good to know." His smile swept across both women.

Tessy wished he stay focused on her just a little more, but it'd be rude to exclude Mama. Jeremiah didn't strike her as a person who would ever be rude.

He held out the pants. "I did soak those last night in the hopes of coaxin' out a bit of the soda." Grinning, he turned his attention to Tessy. "I don't know what they use to make that red color, but it sure is effective. Left the most becomin' shade of pink behind. 'Course, most men aren't too keen on the idea of pink britches."

Tessy's face heated up at his comment. He wasn't intending to berate her for her clumsiness yesterday, but the embarrassment still burned in her chest. She swung her face away so he wouldn't read her eyes.

"'Course, pink in the cheeks of a pretty girl, now that's a completely different thing." His voice pulled softly from behind her, and she heard Mama titter. "Wouldn't you agree, Mrs. McCleary, that a blushin' girl is one of the prettiest sights on God's earth?"

Tessy peeked at Mama's beaming smile.

"Oh, I agree completely, Preacher. I imagine God gave women the ability to blush just to brighten things up a bit." Mama's impish response was out of character for her normally reserved demeanor. What kind of effect did this man have on people?

Tessy's gaze wandered to Jeremiah, finding him waiting for her to look at him.

His broad grin nearly melted her heart. "Yes, I'd say it's definitely true. Nothin' prettier on God's earth…"

His words left Tessy feeling as if she floated above the grass. She knew about flirting from watching other young folks engage in the activity, but she'd never had anyone involve her in the sport. Jeremiah's attention flustered her, but it was also heady to be the recipient of such consideration. She wished she knew how to respond. All she could do was stand there stupidly with her cheeks flaming fiery hot while Mama appeared as enamored with Jeremiah as Tessy felt.

"Well, now, young man, hand over those britches so I can get them through the wash water." Mama reached out her chapped hands.

Tessy leapt between the two and snatched the pants from Jeremiah. "Huh-uh." Her own brazenness brought a fresh rush of heat. "I got 'em dirty, I'll get 'em clean again." Then she faltered, looking from one stunned face to the other. But a grin sneaked up Jeremiah's cheek, bringing that single dimple into view, and Tessy answered it with a grin of her own. "That is, if you trust me not to make a mess of it."

Jeremiah raised one hand and placed his fingertips on Tessy's arm. The gentle pressure of his fingers on her flesh brought an immediate tingle of response. "I trust you, Tessy."

Those words, so sincerely spoken, touched Tessy more deeply than anything he could have said. She sensed the meaning extended beyond the care of his trousers, and tears stung behind her eyes. No one had ever trusted Tessy McCleary before. No one. Except Ol' Gordy, and in the town's eyes he wouldn't even count. But Jeremiah would count.

"I—I'll bring 'em back to you this evening. After they've dried an' I've run an iron over 'em."

Jeremiah laughed, a deep belly rumble that set Tessy's heart to pattering like grease popping in a pan. "Ironing's not necessary, Tessy. Once I strap the braces over the top of my pants legs, they get all wrinkly anyway. Clean is good enough for me."

Tessy nodded, appreciating the easy acceptance of his braces. Jeremiah liked himself just the way he was, and she found herself wishing she could be as comfortable in her own skin as he seemed to be in his. "Then I'll bring 'em to you this evening after they're clean."

Jeremiah gave another smiling nod to her mother. "Good-bye now, Mrs. McCleary. Thanks so much for taking care of this for me." His gaze returned to Tessy, and his eyes softened. "And thank you, Tessy. I'll see you later."

Tessy smiled her answer, unable to find her voice, lost once more in the depths of his kind, blue eyes. He turned and moved away, the familiar hitch somehow having endeared itself to Tessy in the short time she'd known him.

"Now that's a very nice young man," Mama said, and Tessy swung to find Mama peering at her speculatively. "And he seems quite taken with you, daughter."

Tessy crushed his trousers against her front. "It's a good feelin', Mama, to have a man like that pay kindness to me, but makes me kind of scared, too."

"Scared?" Mama scrubbed an apron against the washboard, her brows pulled down. "Now what about Preacher Jeremiah Hatcher could scare you?"

"Everything." She didn't share the rest with her mother, but inside her heart cried. She liked Jeremiah Hatcher more than anyone she'd ever met. And of course the more one liked something, the more it hurt when it was suddenly gone. It wouldn't take long and Jeremiah would be gone. He was only here to do Pop's job while Pop was down to bed. Even if he didn't turn away like the rest of the town had, he wasn't here for good. He'd be leaving. The fear of the heartache that was sure to come at his parting was the biggest fear of all.

Jeremiah spent most of the afternoon on the Winters' porch with his Bible in his lap, preparing for Sunday's sermon. His studying suffered several interruptions as he paused to greet the patients who came and went. Holden did a fairly steady business, and since his office was right off the front porch, Jeremiah was privy to every ache and pain experienced by the townspeople by the time the day was finished. Nearly every person requested a prayer of healing for them, and he refused none of them.

Jeremiah laughed when Holden overheard the requests and said with a wry grin, "Doesn't say much for their confidence in my doctoring when they ask you to pray for them as they're leaving my office."

Jeremiah had replied, tongue in cheek, "Look at it as their way of making me feel useful."

He needed to feel useful. The years in Russia and Poland during the war had been years of heartache, of constantly feeling as if he couldn't do enough. Then he'd gotten sick and they'd sent him home before the task was finished. Right now, across the ocean, battles were waging, children were suffering, families were dying. And here sat Jeremiah on a porch swing, unable to do anything to help.

The overwhelming burden of guilt for failing to help more Jewish people escape Hitler's madness was a weight that threatened to bury him at times. Sitting here, listening to these mountain people share their troubles, being trusted to lift their cares before the Heavenly Father, helped soothe the frayed edges of Jeremiah's tattered heart. Praying for them was healing for himself. He delighted in it.

The supper hour was nearly upon them when the gate hinges squeaked and Jeremiah looked up from his Bible to see Tessy McCleary step hesitantly into the yard. She held a brown-paper wrapped bundle tied with white string, and her hair was pulled back in a simple tail with a bit of the same plain string. Jeremiah smiled. Tessy's natural beauty needed no embellishments. His heart lifted at the sight of her.

"Hello, Tessy." He closed his Bible and took the package as she stepped onto the porch. "You finished earlier than I expected. Thank you."

"You're welcome, Jeremiah." She pointed to the package. "All the pink came out. No one 'll ever know that strawberry Nehi ran down your leg."

Jeremiah patted the paper, making it crackle. "Oh, but every time I wear these, I'll remember how I tried to treat you to a soda and got a shower instead." He smiled and winked, letting her know he was teasing. "And I'll also remember that I still owe you a strawberry Nehi."

Tessy's gray eyes widened. "You don't owe me nothing."

"You didn't get to drink that one, so the way I look at it, I still owe you." She shook her head slightly, but before she could offer another argument, he said, "Would you care to sit down for a bit?"

"Sit?" She blinked, her gray eyes unreadable.

Jeremiah's cheek muscles twitched with the effort of holding back a chuckle. "Uh-huh, sit. You know, bend your legs and put yourself in the chair..." She continued to stand and stare at him with that same blank expression. What on earth was she thinking? He added, "Unless, of course, you still have laundry to do."

Finally she shook her head, seeming to break out of the stupor. "Laundry's all done."

She worked her thumbs back and forth along each fingertip. A nervous habit, he was sure. How could he put her at ease? "Then come sit and visit with me. I've been inhaling a wonderful scent, and I can't recognize it. Maybe you can tell me what it is."

Tessy gingerly seated herself on the edge of the rocking chair, planted her bare feet side-by-side, and smoothed her blue checked skirt over her knees. She sniffed, her head tipped to the side, then a smile of recognition crossed her face. "Breeze is from the east. You're smellin' forget-me-nots. A whole passel of 'em grow in the yard beside Doc and Callie's house." She turned backward and pointed. Jeremiah leaned, too, and peered at the side yard. "See all them little blue flowers with a hint of yellow at the throat?"

Jeremiah spotted clusters of blue faces varying from light to dark, growing on fragile stems that reached barely higher than a trimmed grass blade. "Yes, I see them."

"Them are called dwarfs, 'cause they're smaller than most forget-me-nots, but the size don't seem to matter when it comes to fragrance. They produce a rich scent, don't you think?" A smile lit her face. "White ones grow in the peaks, and even if you can't see 'em, you can smell 'em long before you come upon 'em. Not many smells better than a bed of forget-me-nots."

Jeremiah leaned back into the swing, causing the chains to twang. "Forget-me-nots..." He nodded, swallowing a grin as he attempted a serious face. "I think I can remember that."

Tessy's face flooded with color. She bounced to her feet. "I best get home and help Mama with supper. Nice talkin' with you, Preacher...um, Jeremiah."

Before he had a chance to reply, she skipped down the steps, out the gate, and disappeared down the footpath. Jeremiah turned a puzzled gaze in her direction, wondering why she had so quickly departed. Then the sound of a clearing throat caught his attention, and he turned to find a husky, late-forties man standing at the far end of the picket fence. The brim of a tan cowboy hat shadowed all but his chin, which thrust out in a belligerent manner.

"You the new preacher?" The man's voice carried the weight of authority.

Jeremiah nodded, straightening his legs and reaching to snap the knee locks.

The fellow entered the yard uninvited and strode to the steps. He planted one large foot on the second riser and rested his hand on his raised knee. "Don't bother to get up. I'm Colt Murphy, mayor of Shyler's Point. Also serve as law enforcement." His chest seemed to puff with the last statement.

Jeremiah leaned forward as far as he could and stuck out his hand to give Colt Murphy a firm handshake. "It's nice to meet you, Mr. Murphy."

"Call me Colt." He nearly crushed Jeremiah's fingers with the strength of his grip.

"Colt." Jeremiah settled back into the swing. "Can I

do something for you?"

Colt removed his hat, revealing a thick thatch of steel gray hair, and bounced it against his thigh. "You can tell me how long that McCleary girl was sitting here with you."

What business was that of this man, even if he was the mayor? Jeremiah scratched his chin. "Not too long. She brought me some clean laundry." He patted the package resting on the swing seat beside him. "Why do you ask?"

Colt Murphy took a deep breath, clapped the hat onto his head, and pulled the brim low. He peered at Jeremiah with narrowed eyes. "'Cause about an hour ago, Miz Nancy Kirby reported the theft of a wicker handbag from the kitchen counter inside her back porch door. An' she says Tessy McCleary took it."

7

"I'm sorry, Jeremiah." Callie dished healthy servings of shepherd's pie onto willow ware plates and handed them around the table. "Holden or I should have mentioned the thefts that have been happening around town the past several months. If I'd had any idea that Colt would stop by and dump the problem in your lap, I would have made sure I mentioned it."

"It did come as a shock." Jeremiah was still reeling from his brief conversation with the town's law enforcement official. "I probably stammered like an idiot, but there wasn't anything I could tell him other than no, I didn't see a handbag, and yes, Tessy did seem nervous. When I mentioned that I don't know Tessy very well but it's my impression that she's always nervous, he didn't seem to care much."

Holden released a sigh. "I would imagine the whole town knows about Nancy's run-in with Tessy at the general store yesterday. People like to talk. I'm sure Nancy assumed Tessy took that handbag as a way of getting even for the way she snapped at her over the spilled soda."

Jeremiah shook his head. "I still maintain that Tessy is too timid to go around extracting revenge. I watched her reaction in the store. She gave no appearance of anger, only regret. I admit, I wanted to give the clerk a piece of my mind over the way she treated Tessy, but Tessy apologized and moved on." He paused, worry striking. "You don't think Nancy actually saw Tessy take it, do you?"

"It wouldn't matter if she didn't." Callie took hold of Holden's hand as she sat in her chair. "No one has *seen* Tessy take anything. But, oddly enough, each time a theft occurs, it follows some sort of altercation between Tessy and the owner of the stolen item. The other strange part is the items are never of real monetary value, but of personal significance. As far as anyone around here is concerned, that's proof enough. If something turns up missing, they blame Tessy because a jinx would take something to hurt the person's heart more than her bank account."

"This just gets worse and worse." Jeremiah crossed his arms in disgust. "First she's a jinx, now she's a jinx *and* a thief? Don't these narrow-minded people have anything better to do than cast stones?"

Callie and Holden exchanged a meaningful look.

Jeremiah hung his head. "Please forgive me. I was

judgmental and very unchristian. I'm just overwhelmed right now." Part of his fury was aimed at what he had witnessed over the past several years. Hitler's unfair treatment of the Jewish people was a sore that continued to fester. Now he seemed to be reliving it, to a small degree, watching a community unfairly brand one of its members as an outcast. While their mistreatment of Tessy was not nearly as severe as what Hitler had perpetrated against the Jews, it was unmerited, and it stung Jeremiah's tender heart.

Callie patted his hand. "You're forgiven. Jeremiah, I admire your willingness to stand up for Tessy. That says a lot about your character."

He sensed there was more she wanted to say. "But…?"

She offered a sad smile. "But be careful, please? The superstitious beliefs aren't taken lightly around here, and the people might not respond kindly to an outsider who comes raging through and stomps on their toes about things they've believed since childhood. Tread carefully, will you?"

Jeremiah reared back in surprise. "Are you telling me to be cautious when I step into the pulpit?"

Color increased in Callie's cheeks, but she shrugged. "I can't tell you what to preach. If God instructs you to speak out on superstition, I won't stand in your way. But please don't use the pulpit as your own battleground against it, either. These mountain people are tenacious—

they've had to be to survive in the hills where carving out a living is anything but easy. They tend to be just as tenacious in their beliefs. Even though you're a man of God, which warrants respect, you can make enemies if you move too quickly, speak too harshly. At least at first." She sighed. "I suppose what I'm asking is for you to prayerfully consider the stand you plan to make before you act on it."

Jeremiah appreciated Callie's candor. "I always prayerfully consider my sermons before I speak."

"Good." Callie swung her gaze to Holden. "Now, say grace before everything is cold."

Holden obliged, and the conversation turned to other topics. But Jeremiah found it difficult to concentrate. He kept thinking about Colt Murphy's certainty that Tessy had taken Nancy Kirby's purse. He remembered Tessy's nervous behavior and her rapid departure when the mayor had appeared. Was she nervous because she was guilty of stealing? She hadn't been carrying a purse, but she could have hidden it before she delivered his laundry.

He gave himself a mental kick. He would not be pulled into this nonsense. The laws of the land dictated that a person was innocent until proven guilty. Until he had proof staring him in the face, he would believe Tessy was innocent of wrong-doing. He'd always been a good judge of character. The ability had served him well when choosing people to help with his work in Europe. His instincts now told him Tessy was not a thief despite what the community thought. Until he had concrete evidence proving otherwise, he would staunchly defend Tessy's innocence. Someone had to be reasonable in this town full of irrational people.

On Sunday morning, Jeremiah took his place behind the simple pulpit in the Mountainside Bible Church. Looking out on the congregation—at their upturned, open faces—he found it difficult to believe these people could be so attentive and receptive in church, yet coldly reject one of their own the moment church was over.

He had chosen First John, chapter four, for his text. As he read the familiar verses — "'...Ye are of God, little children, and have overcome the world: because greater is he that is in you, than he that is in the world... Beloved, let us love one another; for love is of God; and every one that loveth is born of God, and knoweth God... Beloved, if God so loved us, we ought also to love one another... And this commandment have we from him, That he who loveth God love his brother also...'"—his heart beat in hopefulness that the underlying message would break through without him raising a finger of accusation. Callie's concerned warning weighed heavily on his shoulders. He didn't want to make enemies here, he wanted to unite the community as one body.

As Jeremiah expounded on the verses, breaking the chapter into pieces and sharing the message God had laid upon his heart, he was keenly aware of Tessy in the same spot he'd seen her the first night here—front row, at the end near the wall. A well-worn Bible lay, unopened, in her lap. She kept her gaze riveted to his, seemingly absorbing every word. He found it difficult not to single her out with extra attention, so intent was her concentration.

He deliberately moved his gaze across the congregation, making eye contact with each person at some point during the message. They seemed receptive to his words, and his heart lifted with hope. As he spoke, he inwardly prayed for them to realize their error and accept Tessy completely into their fold.

"And so once we have become a part of God's family, we have truly become brothers and sisters in God's eyes. We are adopted heirs with Jesus Christ, children of the Heavenly Father. Thus the words we read in verses 20 and 21 are a message from our Father to us: 'If a man say, I love God, and hateth his brother, he is a liar: for he that loveth not his brother whom he hath seen, how can he love God whom he hath not seen? And this commandment have we from him, That he who loveth God loveth his brother also.' It is my prayer that you carry those words on your heart, and you recall them as you meet each another in the streets of Shyler's Point. Let's show God our love for Him by freely caring for one another.

Shall we pray?"

After the closing prayer, Holden came forward and led the congregation in a hymn. When the song was finished, Jeremiah made his way to the double doors of the church to shake hands and bid a farewell to the attendees. Although most comments were rather generic— "Thank you, Preacher, for the message," or "You got a good speakin' voice, Preacher"—he still held out hope he would see a change in attitude in at least a few of the people.

Tessy was one of the last ones to exit. He glimpsed her hovering in the entryway, appearing to hold back until everyone else had gone. Jeremiah thought she looked especially nice in a her yellow dress with the white collar, her honey-colored hair pulled back and held with a white satin ribbon. She wore shoes for the occasion—simple white pumps with a strap that buttoned across the instep. The heels gave her added height which seemed to accentuate her slender build. Jeremiah was sure his smile broadened when she approached and placed her hand into his.

"You did a real fine job, Preacher." She tipped her head and fixed him with a steady look. "Seemed real at home up there at that pulpit. Figure God knew what He was doing when He called you to speak."

Her words warmed him more than any others. "Thank you, Tessy. That means a lot to me."

She closed her eyes for a moment, her hand motionless within his. "'…if God so loved us, we ought also to love one another.'" She sighed and opened her gray eyes to meet his gaze again. "Powerful words."

"I didn't write them, you know. I just read them."

She smiled. "And you did that real good, too." She withdrew her hand with a little start. "I—I better get home now." She turned and skipped down the steps. But halfway to the bottom she stopped and looked back over her shoulder, her expression thoughtful. "You know, Jeremiah, it's too bad the world leaders didn't hear your sermon. Maybe if they all could follow what God wrote in His Book, the war would stop right away."

Jeremiah nodded, fighting a lump in his throat.

She hurried across the yard, her pony tail seeming to wave goodbye. He stood looking after her until Callie and Holden emerged. As they walked slowly toward the Winters' home, Jeremiah looked at Callie. "Did I step on toes, do you think?"

Callie smirked. "Ah, Jeremiah, you are subtle. I recognized your ploy, but you were so clever in your preaching, I'm sure no one else caught the message below the surface."

Jeremiah frowned. "Meaning no one will go home, look in the mirror, and wonder if they should make some changes?"

"Not at all." Callie patted his arm. "If they truly listened, of course they will examine their own hearts and see if they lack the kind of love you spoke of this morning. But you presented the information in such a caring, personable manner, no one could find insult hiding in the message."

"I suppose that's a good thing." But had he been forceful enough to make an impact? So much needed changing here in Shyler's Point. He released a brief snort. Much needed changing everywhere in the world. Although Hitler was now dead—killed by his own hand—and his reign of terror was over, the Japanese still waged war with the United States. Things were not calm no matter how peaceful the appearance the setting in which he now walked.

Holden held open the gate for Jeremiah and Callie to enter the yard, and Callie gave a slight groan as she climbed the stairs. She paused at the top, clutching her belly with both hands and letting her head drop back.

Holden moved quickly past Jeremiah and put his arm around her waist. "What is it?"

The hair on the back of Jeremiah's neck prickled at the concern in Holden's voice.

Callie sent a smile in Holden's direction. "Your very busy offspring is making his or her presence known. Sometimes I wish the baby didn't kick so hard. It hurts!"

"Just a kick?" Holden scowled. "Not a contraction?"

Callie placed her hand along Holden's jaw. "Not a

contraction, Holden. Just a kick. Stop worrying." She shook her finger playfully in Jeremiah's direction. "You, too. One worrier in this house is enough. Come on. I'll get dinner on the table."

Holden caught her hand. "Let us do that."

Callie shook her head. "Huh-uh. I'll let you wait on me hand and foot after this baby is born, but until then, let me do as I please. It'll take my mind off the little foot that is trying to push its way between my ribs." She pranced into the house, leaving the two men on the porch.

Holden released a huff. "Women. Mark my words, Jeremiah, when you get married, find a woman who doesn't have a stubborn bone in her body. Your life will be much easier."

Jeremiah couldn't help the grin tugging at his cheek. He'd witnessed enough of the relationship between the Winters to know that Holden loved everything about Callie, including her penchant for independent stubbornness. "I imagine Callie's stubborn streak is like seasoning in a stew. She'd be pretty bland without it."

Holden clapped Jeremiah on the shoulder. "You're right, my friend. I retract my original statement. I hope you find a woman exactly like my Callie. I guarantee you will find happiness wrapped in the bundle."

Holden went into the house, but Jeremiah clumped to the swing. Unhooking the knee locks on his braces, he lowered himself to the wooden seat and gave it a gentle push. He breathed deeply, inhaling the sweet scent of the forget-me-nots, letting his eyes drift closed as he reflected on what Holden had said.

God, what's Your plan for me concerning a family? I'm already twenty-nine. How much longer will I have to wait?

He opened his eyes to a flash of white. Sunlight sneaking between the porch railings reflected on the silver brace protecting his leg. He winced against the brightness, shifting slightly to avoid blinding himself. He'd reconciled himself to his handicap years ago. Despite being slowed down physically, he had been able to fulfill his call to become a minister. He'd even traveled to parts of the world none of his brothers had seen. So why did the reminder of those silver braces make him wonder if he could become a husband and father?

Heaviness weighted his chest as he considered the sacrifice a woman would make to become his wife. The man should protect the wife, to be the leader, and Jeremiah believed this meant the man should be the stronger one both spiritually and physically. He slapped at his leg brace in frustration.

Was marriage out of the question for him? If so, God would have to give him peace, remove the longing for family from his heart, and help him see his ministry as enough.

A cardinal sang from the overgrown spirea bushes alongside the house. He whistled with the bird, reminding himself of his purpose in Shyler's Point. He'd come to preach and to recover. And now it seemed God was giving him the additional task of helping Tessy.

A smile tugged at his lips, ending his whistling tune. She'd focused so intently on the sermon that morning. The image didn't match a person who would steal from and intentionally create havoc for her neighbors. How could he help free Tessy from the bonds of suspicion and resentment in which the town had imprisoned her?

Prove her innocent.

The thought jolted him. If he could prove without a doubt that Tessy was not the one stealing items, then the town would have to acknowledge they were wrong in seeing her as a thief. Then he could convince them they had also been wrong about her being a jinx.

Excitement built in his chest. If he could catch the real thief, or at the very least provide an honest alibi for Tessy, it would disprove the accusations. Then he could work at erasing the ludicrous superstitious belief that Tessy was a jinx. He curled his fingers around the edge of the seat, prepared to launch into action.

Again the braces caught the sun. As quickly as his heart had lifted, it now fell like a rock into the pit of his stomach. Who was he trying to fool? How could he possibly play detective with these uncooperative legs? Did he think he could chase down a real thief caught in the act, or traipse after Tessy on her long jaunts to verify she wasn't victimizing her fellow townspeople?

He hadn't complained about his braces since he was a boy of twelve and left out of a schoolyard baseball game, but at that moment he would have given anything to throw them off and walk strong and fast like other men.

"Jeremiah? Lunch is ready." Callie called from inside the house.

"I'm coming." Straightening his legs, he clicked the locks into position and then struggled to his feet. "I'm coming…slowly, but surely." As he reached for the screen door, a thought struck him.

Slowly, but surely… God had never let him down when he prayed and asked for help in meeting the goals he had set for himself. Why would God hold him back now? Nothing was impossible for God—not even a crippled man catching a thief. Jeremiah was working on the side of right. God would certainly honor that with success. His heart winged into his chest once more.

As he crossed through the parlor to the kitchen, his confidence grew. He and God could do it. He would start his detective work tomorrow, bright and early.

Dust motes shimmered like flakes of gold, and she found herself humming softly as her feet crossed almost silently over the thick, mossy ground. There were deer paths where the ground was exposed, leaving behind a narrow, smooth pathway, but Tessy preferred to find her own way through the forest areas. It was like an adventure to seek out new ways of reaching familiar favorite spots.

Her gaze bounced from the delicate yellow butterfly weed to patches of purple phlox and blue lobelia. Deep green ferns grew around the flowering plants, providing a perfect backdrop for the colorful blossoms. Tessy marveled at the variety of plants flourishing in the shade of the forests. God had surely used His creativity when He put together these mountains. Her eyes feasted on every color of the rainbow and every variation in between.

Stepping from the trees, she hop-skipped over rocks and mosses to the bank of the Little Muddy. She moved to a large, smooth rock on the south shore—a perfect vantage point for the dam on the opposite side. Seating herself on the warm surface, she popped off her shoes and then dipped her feet in the water. At the first cold splash across her bare toes, she laughed with delight, thrusting her feet clear to the ankles into the sparkling water.

Lady slippers in a variety of colors bloomed profusely along the bank, with yellow fringed and purple fringeless orchids—the latter's rich red-purple bloom eliciting a sigh of pleasure from her lips—rearing their regal heads farther upstream. She reached for her pack, removing pencils and paper, as she talked to the flowers.

"Oh, you beautiful purple fringeless, when I'm done with the beavers, I'll come draw you. But don't know how I can ever put on paper your true beauty." Sighing again, she turned her gaze from the orchids to the beaver's conglomeration of sticks and mud. She giggled. "Mr. Beaver, I can't hardly call your home beautiful, but I admire your workmanship."

She bent over her paper, pencil in hand, and began sketching. Keeping her chin low, she raised her eyes to peer at the dam, then quickly looked back at the paper, recreating what she saw with deft strokes of the lead. Occasionally she stopped to sharpen the pencil with her pocketknife, her movements quick and stern, irritated with the interruption, then she squinted at the dam and continued drawing.

The river burbled merrily. The beavers splashed in and out of the water, their conversational grumblings carrying across the creek to Tessy's ears. The sun beat hot and steady on her head. She lost herself in the pleasure of moving the colored pencils over the paper where slowly a detailed image of the beavers' dam emerged.

She was reaching for her black pencil to do some shading at the base of the dam when the large, male beaver suddenly slapped his tail against the water and all three animals dove below the surface. Tessy raised her head, trepidation causing gooseflesh to break out across her arms. What had frightened the animals? Then somewhere behind her, she heard the *snap* of a twig breaking.

Her feet sent out a spray of water as she jerked them out of the river. Pencils rolled off the rock and landed in the moss at its base as she spun to see what was behind her. At once, her fear gave way to relief, but heat climbed her cheeks. She pressed her drawing pad against the bodice of her dress. "Jeremiah." Her heart beat so hard she found it difficult to speak his name. "I thought you might be a black bear sneakin' up on me."

His familiar smile warmed her more than the sun. He closed the remaining gap between them, his crutch catching on moss as he struggled across the uneven ground. When he stood next to her, he placed his palms on the sturdy top surface of the rock, then lowered himself to sit on it, his legs sticking straight out in front of him. He laid the crutch on the ground beside the rock and released a long sigh.

"Whew! That was quite a trek." His gaze roved up and down the river, his face creased in pleasure. "And well worth it. What a beautiful spot. Do you come here often?"

She sat looking at him stupidly, still crushing her pad to her chest. What was he doing up here? "I... Um..." How disconcerting to be alone on the mountain with this handsome minister.

"You didn't really think I was a bear, did you?" His eyes widened, as if he'd found the answer without her speaking. "I'm so sorry, Tessy. I didn't mean to frighten you."

Tessy finally found her voice. "It's okay. My mind was focused on other things. An' I wasn't expectin' anybody to come along, so when those beavers jumped under the water…" Realizing she was rambling, she stopped and swallowed hard, then finished lamely, "Mostly I'm alone out here."

Mostly she was alone? Always she was alone, unless she came across Ol' Gordy. Having Jeremiah's companionship was just as good. Or maybe even better. "What are you doin' out here?" She scooted over to give him more room on the rock settee.

He gave a slight shrug. "I've wandered through most of the town. I wanted to get a glimpse of the surrounding countryside. You live in a beautiful area."

She nodded, his words nearly echoing what she had thought earlier as she'd walked to Little Muddy.

Jeremiah's gaze dropped to Tessy's crossed arms, and his brows pulled down in curiosity. "What have you got there?"

Tessy glanced at her drawing pad. What would she would do if he asked to look at it? Only Ol' Gordy had seen her drawings. She licked her lips. "Just my picture book."

Jeremiah tipped his head, his gaze sweeping over the scattered pencils at the base of the rock. A grin spread across his face. "A picture book that you made yourself?"

She nodded, unconsciously tightening her arms on the pad.

He shifted and pointed at the dam. "That's quite an accomplishment for the furry creatures."

Tessy smiled in relief, glad for the change in subject. "Beavers are very…industrious." She felt wise, saying a word Pete would use.

"I haven't seen a beaver dam since I was a boy, and it was considerably smaller than this one." Jeremiah, gaze on the dam, slid his palms on the rock. His right hand came very near her left knee.

Her stomach fluttered like a Monarch butterfly had been set loose in there. "It's one of my favorite things in the forest." Her voice wavered. She wanted to relax, to enjoy his company, but her tummy did such funny things when he was near. She jabbered to cover her discomfort. "I'm glad to see the beavers makin' a return. Shyler's Point was started when the first Mr. Spencer built a fur trading post on the ridge. Mostly he traded for beaver, but also some bear, otter, and fox. French fur trappers nearly wiped out the beavers to make fancy hats. But a handful of the beavers survived, and the traders moved on, so now the animals are free to build their dams in peace. Unless"—she shrugged—"someone like you or me comes along an' disturbs them."

"I don't think you disturbed them." Jeremiah sent her a crinkling grin. "They seemed very comfortable in your presence. My clumsiness scared them back into the water." He frowned, his gaze returning to the dam. "Speaking of which, do you think they'll surface soon? I wouldn't want them to drown."

Tessy laughed. "They're snug in their den right now, not in the water at all. They'll lay low and listen, an' when they feel safe, they'll come out again. If we stay quiet, we'll get to see them."

Jeremiah blew out a little breath. "Oh, good. I'd hate to be responsible for the demise of some of the few beavers remaining in Shyler's Point."

Her heart stirred with another reason to like Jeremiah Hatcher. She loved the woodland creatures, but she hadn't realized that a man would care more for the animal than what its fur could bring. She wished she could gift him. He'd seemed open to her talking about the beaver, so she offered a bit more of her knowledge.

She pointed to the bank behind the dam. "See that dark spot in the bank? What looks like a small cave?"

Jeremiah leaned forward, shielding his eyes with his hand. "Yes."

"Sometimes, if the water's too deep, beavers'll burrow in a riverbank and not even build a dam. That's where these beavers lived before they built their dam here on the Little Muddy. There'll be a nice den in the bank, with another opening underwater." She tipped her head, leaning a bit closer, gesturing with one hand while keeping a grip on her drawing pad with the other. "They build from under the water, burrowing upward an' then hollowing out the den before digging out to the opening we see. That way they aren't without shelter."

She sighed, smiling at a memory. "It's a fine thing to watch a whiskered face emergin' from the bank, like a chick burstin' from an egg." Jeremiah's smile urged her to continue. "Clever critters, ain't they? And now that they've got their dam all fixed up, some other critter will come along and move into the abandoned den."

He stared at her in seeming amazement.

Tessy licked her lips. "What…what's wrong?"

"Nothing is wrong." He shook his head as if arguing with himself about something. "You know a lot about beavers."

She shrugged. "Know about lots of critters. My granny taught me about the woods and its wild things. An' Ol' Gordy—" She clapped her hand over her mouth. Ol' Gordy didn't like her talking about him with other people.

"Old Gordy…?"

Tessy turned away. The beady black eyes of a beaver poked above the water in front of the dam. She pointed silently. Jeremiah looked, and a broad smile broke across his face. He swung his gaze to her, gave a wink, then turned back to the beavers. They sat for a few minutes watching the animals return to work. The beavers reminded Tessy of little men as they waddled over the mound with their stiff tails dragging, using their deft front paws to push and twist the twigs that shaped the dam.

After several minutes, Jeremiah leaned toward Tessy and whispered, "Were you drawing the beaver's dam when I came along and startled you?"

Her fingers convulsed around the edge of the drawing pad. Her gaze on the dam, she nodded slowly. She peeked out of the corner of her eyes. Jeremiah's blue-eyed gaze had settled on her.

His lips tipped up sweetly. "May I see it?"

She'd kept her picture-drawing a secret out of fear that others would poke fun at her. Her heart told her she could trust Jeremiah, but years of holding back were hard to overcome.

"If you'd rather not share, I'll understand." His soft, sincere voice was as gentle as the patter of summer rain. She knew he wouldn't hold a grudge if she said no, but suddenly she wanted him to see her picture. She wanted to share the secret side of herself with him, to show him there was some good inside of her.

Very slowly she pulled the pad away from her chest. She looked at it first, her gaze roving from top to bottom.

It wasn't finished—it still needed some shading—but it was close. She swallowed, took a deep breath, and turned the pad around.

Jeremiah's gaze dropped to the drawing. His eyes widened. A pleased smile climbed his cheeks. "You drew this?" Holding out his hand, he silently requested the pad.

She handed it over, her heart pounding. She held her breath as he placed the pad in his lap and carefully examined the picture, his finger tracing the shape of the dam and trailing over to touch the dark spot in the bank behind it.

"Tessy, this is absolutely beautiful. Why, it's like looking at a photograph. I had no idea you were so talented."

Tessy's breath whooshed out. His words were even better than Ol' Gordy's praise. Tessy felt as if someone had lit a candle and thrust it into her middle, lighting her from within. The pleasure made her shiver, and she hugged herself, savoring the glory of the moment.

"You could sell this drawing. It's every bit as good as the plates I've seen in encyclopedias and other published books."

"Published books?" Her voice squeaked. Her heart thrummed in sudden fearful shame.

"Yes." Jeremiah continued examining the drawing. "Absolutely amazing…"

Tessy couldn't sell the picture. Jeremiah needed to

know why before he got carried away with his idea. But how to tell him? The weight pressed at her chest, filling her with disgrace. What would he think of her when he knew? But she had to tell him. Then he'd give up the notion.

She twisted her fingers together in her lap. "If…if that picture was to appear in a real book, what would it say on the page? There's always some writin' at the bottom, underneath the pictures in books."

"What's the name of this river?"

"Little Muddy."

He gave a brisk nod. "Then it would probably say something like, 'Beaver dam at Little Muddy River' underneath."

She picked up one of the fallen pencils and held it out to him. It quivered. Her whole body went damp with perspiration. "Jeremiah, would—would you please write the words at the bottom of the page for me?"

His head shot up, his thick brows coming together. Then his jaw dropped slightly, indicating his understanding.

Tessy wished she could climb under the rock on which she sat. Now he knew.

9

When Jeremiah had spotted Tessy walking behind the general store this morning, he'd followed her to prove she wasn't sneaking off to someone's house to take something that didn't belong to her. Since her feet were more sure than his, he'd struggled to keep up. Twice he thought he lost her. His relief was great when he spotted her on this rock in the sun.

Tessy's vast knowledge of the beavers surprised him. Her simple words and homey way of phrasing intimated simplicity of thinking, but now he knew that to be untrue. She obviously carried a great deal of knowledge about the woods' plant and animal life.

The sketch pad gave a second surprise. He could hardly believe how intricately each minute detail of the dam was presented on the page. He could probably count the sticks in the dam and compare it to the drawing, and it would be an accurate representation.

But this last revelation surprised him the most. Tessy couldn't write. It therefore followed she couldn't read. A brilliant older brother who was a professor in a college, and Tessy was illiterate. His heart ached for her. How insignificant she must feel. And she had shared the truth with him. What a privilege to be privy to her secret pain.

"Yes. I'll write it for you." His voice sounded strange, hollow, and he cleared his throat, trying to swallow the bubble of sadness threatening to choke him. He took the pencil and very carefully printed the words along the bottom edge of the page. When he handed the pad to her, she took it reverently, turning it and running her finger below the words. Her lips formed the phrase, but no sound came out.

"Tessy?" He waited until she lifted her face to him. The sadness in her gray eyes pierced him. "Would you like to learn to write the words for yourself?"

Her face lit with eagerness, and then just as quickly the expression changed to despair. She dropped her chin. "I could never learn."

"Why not?"

She shook her head, her golden hair swinging like a silk curtain around her cheeks.

"Tessy, look at me."

She raised her face and pinned her sorrowful gaze on his.

"Why not?"

"'Cause I'm too dumb." Tears glittered in her eyes. "I couldn't learn when I was little, and I'm too old to learn now."

Jeremiah's pulse increase. Part sympathy, part anger. Certainly the town's treatment had played a part in convincing Tessy she was incapable of learning. He wished to soothe away the long-held hurts and help this woman see herself for the beautiful person she truly was.

He took a deep breath, winging heavenward a silent prayer for wisdom. "If I ask you a question, will you be honest with me?" He waited for her nod. "You and I don't know each other very well, but I need to know if you trust me."

Tessy's face flooded with pink, her eyes grew even wider, and she straightened her shoulders in surprise. "You're a preacher, Jeremiah. Of course I trust you."

He shook his head. "I'm not asking if you trust me as a preacher. I'm asking if you trust me as a friend."

"A—a friend?" She seemed to roll the word from her tongue, as if experimenting with its sound and flavor. Tipping her head, she looked past his shoulder for a moment, appearing to give the question deep consideration. Finally she brought her gaze back to him, her expression solemn. "Yes. I believe I trust you as... as a friend."

Given her obvious lack of friendships in the community and just cause to distrust people, he found it heart lifting that she could find the courage to offer her trust.

He vowed never to give her reason to regret the offer. "Then I want you to believe me when I tell you something. You are not dumb. You can learn. It's a matter of whether you want to badly enough." He maintained eye contact, the conviction in his voice strong.

She hung her head. "If I'm able to learn, how come I didn't figure it out when I was little, like all the other kids?"

Jeremiah recalled all Callie told him about Tessy not attending school often. He didn't want to make Tessy think he'd been asking questions about her—it could frighten her. He placed his hand over hers. "Did you go to school every day when you were little, like the other kids?"

Her face puckered. "Mama kept me out a lot 'cause I had lots of coughs and colds. Made her nervous to let me go—always scared I'd take real sick. So I didn't go all the time."

"See?" Jeremiah gave her hand a squeeze. "I think what probably happened is that you missed so many days, you lost out on learning. Learning to read and write takes sequence." At her puzzled look, he explained, "You have to learn it in a certain order. It's like climbing stairs. You can't go from the first step to the tenth, can you?"

She smiled. "No, it'd take a mighty leap, an' you'd probably fall and hurt yourself."

Jeremiah laughed. "That's right. You have to take each

step on its own. That's how you learn to read and write—one step at a time." He leaned forward. "Tessy, I believe you can learn. And I'd like to teach you. I'm not a teacher, but I'd like to try. Will you let me?"

She chewed her lip, her brow furrowing. Her shoulders lifted in a shrug, and her eyes showed worry. "I might truly disappoint you, Jeremiah."

He lifted the drawing pad and held it up for her to see. "Look at what you did on this page. Look at the beautiful picture you created. Do you see it? Do you know how few people have the ability to draw like this?" He shook his head. "No, you won't disappoint me. Now, I might disappoint you. You might find out I'm a terrible teacher. But there's only one way for us to know for sure, and that's to give it a try. What do you say?"

Tessy took the drawing pad, closed it, and laid it in her lap. She placed her palms on the smooth cover, her face a study of contemplation. "I like bein' in church, hearing God's Word read out loud. The message slips deep inside me, makes my soul feel peaceful and full."

Jeremiah remembered her rapt, attentive expression during the Sunday services. He'd witnessed peace shining in her eyes.

"If I learned how to read, then I could take out God's Book anytime I wanted to and read what it says. I could get that fullness on my own and not have to wait for church days."

Tears stung behind his eyes at her heartfelt statement. At that moment he wanted Tessy to learn to read more than he wanted to learn to walk again. As badly as he had wanted to save the Jews from destruction in Europe, he wanted to teach her to read. He would not fail at this task.

Her head came up, her eyes shining. "I'd like for you to teach me, if you think you can spare the time." Then worry pinched her features. "How long're you gonna be in Shyler's Point?"

"As long as your father needs me. Until he's on his feet again." Jeremiah expected his stay to be no longer than eight weeks. Suddenly it seemed too short an amount of time to spend with this special young woman.

"Not long," Tessy mused, her gaze turning outward again. "Think it'll be long enough?"

"We'll meet every day," Jeremiah promised. "You'll be reading in no time."

"Every day..." She bit down on her lip again.

Jeremiah scowled. What was troubling her? "Tell me what's wrong." He used his best minister voice—soothing, yet firm.

"I want to learn to read, Jeremiah. Truly I do. An' I believe you'd be a good teacher. But..." Her chin quivered. "Spendin' time with me...ain't always...safe." Her last word was a whisper.

Jeremiah knew what she meant, but he needed her to say it so he could address the issue. "Why not?"

She set her jaw for a moment, squared her shoulders, then blurted, "'Cause I'm a jinx."

Anger built again. He swallowed hard, pushing the emotion back into his belly so he could speak in an even tone. "I don't believe in such things as jinxes. I feel perfectly safe with you. And I want to try to teach you to read." He brushed his palms together to indicate he was finished with that topic. "This is my plan. We'll use the Bible for our school book. I can study for my sermons while you learn how to read. How does that sound?"

Tessy swung to face him, rapt appreciation shining in her eyes. "I'd like that. Thank you."

Her gray eyes sparkled, her honey hair shone in the sun, her face glowed with pleasure. His heart caught at her beauty. His arms ached to embrace her. But embracing her would overstep the boundaries dictated by propriety that separated teacher and pupil, minister and church member. He pressed his palms against his thighs and smiled.

"You're welcome. And there's no time like the present to get started..." He reached inside his shirt pocket and withdrew his small New Testament. "Would you like a lesson now?"

Tessy nodded eagerly.

Although Jeremiah hadn't had time to formulate a plan for teaching Tessy, he knew instinctively he couldn't teach her like a six-year-old child. That would shame her

She tipped her head, her face puckered in query. "Why'd you hug me?"

"Because, Tessy McCleary, you are a gift."

Her lips curved upward even as her brow remained furrowed in puzzlement. Clearly she had no idea what she'd done to please him, but it didn't matter. He knew. It was enough.

Jeremiah opened the Bible again. "Let's look back and see how many other words you can recognize, okay?"

They spent another half hour with Tessy scanning the tiny text, finding the names of God and Jesus, and reading John 4:1 over and over so she could memorize it. "I'm gonna look that up in my own Bible when I get home, and I'll put a line under it. It'll encourage me to keep trying."

"Good idea." Jeremiah grinned. "And I'm going to give you an assignment."

"An assignment?" Tessy leaned back, her face registering horror.

Jeremiah laughed. "Well, certainly. School teachers give assignments, didn't you know that?"

A small smile twitched at her lips. "I guess I didn't."

"It's true. So here's yours. Before tomorrow, I want you to copy the verse John 4:1 onto a piece of paper. Write the words just like you see them in the Bible, and we'll talk about the punctuation and the spelling. Okay?"

Tessy nodded, but she still looked uncertain. "You

sure I can do it? I can write my name, but I haven't done much other writin.'"

Jeremiah picked up the drawing pad and flipped it open, revealing the beaver's dam. "If you can draw with this much detail, you can write letters."

Tessy looked at the drawing. She bit down on her lower lip, but she nodded. "Okay. I'll do my best."

"I know you will."

Tessy lifted her chin to peer at the sky. "Sun's high. Must be dinner time." She looked at him. "Are you hungry?"

He nodded. "Yes. Shall we head back to town?"

Tessy offered a sly smile. "No need. Not if you trust me."

Jeremiah gave her a sideways look. "What are you up to?"

"Stay here an' watch the beavers. I'll be back." She snatched up her empty pack and skipped away, disappearing into the trees.

Instead of doing as she had directed, he closed his eyes in prayer. *God, thank You for bringing me to Shyler's Point. I can't imagine a better place to find peace for my aching heart. Teaching Tessy will be a pleasure for me, I know. Help me find the way to open the door to reading and writing. She wants to learn more about You—I admire that. God, I also ask that You open a door for me. My time in Shyler's Point will go quickly, and then I'll need to*

*move into another position of preaching or whatever else
You have in store for me. Right now I can't seem to think
that far ahead, so please open my eyes and heart to where
You would have me go next. Thank you, Lord...*

He sat quietly, enjoying the sights and sounds of nature. During his last two years in Russia, he'd slept during
the day and crept about at night, delivering food and
clothing to those who were brave enough to harbor Jews.
How wonderful to be out in the middle of the day with
the sun high overhead, to look up and see clouds lazing
instead of the blackness of night. To inhale the glorious
scents of flowers rather than the essence of gun powder
and smoke.

Looking into the sparkling water of the Little Muddy,
he wished he could pop off his shoes and soak his feet as
Tessy had done. Instead, he slid off the rock and leaned to
scoop up handfuls of the cold water and splash himself,
carefully avoiding his braces. He left his shirt dripping,
but the sun would dry him in no time.

The beavers dove back under the water, and he imagined them in their den enjoying a lunch of tree bark. His
stomach growled, and he looked over his shoulder, wishing Tessy would return. The thick stand of pines sent a
quiver through him. But no soldiers would emerge from
these woods. He focused on singing birds and chattering
squirrels, pushing aside the memory of rifle fire and ex-
plosions.

Finally Tessy ambled from the woods, swinging her now bulging pack. Sweat dampened her forehead and her hair hung in uncombed ribbons, but her bright smile invited him to smile broadly in return.

"I got us some lunch." She dropped to her knees beside the rock and dumped the contents of her pack onto the rock's smooth surface. "Wild blackberries and strawberries, watercress, some comfrey leaves, an' wild onions. I'll wash everything in the creek, then we can have a woods picnic."

Jeremiah's hunger fled. Comfrey leaves and wild onions? How would he be able to consume the items she'd scattered across the rock?

Tessy looked up at him, and her smile dimmed. "You okay?"

"Perhaps I'm not as hungry as I originally thought." He didn't want to hurt her feelings, but neither was he willing to eat something recently growing in the woods.

Tessy's eyes sparkled impishly. "You think I'm gonna poison a preacher? That's a surefire way to get kept out of Heaven."

"Not poison, exactly, but…" He must sound ridiculous. There were many edible plants in the woods. His mother had made salads from dandelion greens plucked out of their yard and had filled the soup pot with a variety of green leaves and roots found growing in the areas where he and his brothers played. But they'd eaten those things in his kitchen, where he could be certain they'd been thoroughly washed. They didn't even have plates. What would they put the food on before bringing it to their lips?

Tessy sighed. "If you'd rather we can go back into town an' you can have lunch with Callie an' Doc Winters."

He'd disappointed her. He would eat her woods picnic. After all, he said he trusted her. His cooperation would prove it. "No, that's fine. You get everything…washed… in the Little Muddy." He grimaced. How could anything come clean in a river call Little Muddy?

Tessy burst out laughing. "Jeremiah, your face is turnin' green. I better get you back before you get sick." She scattered the collected food across the ground, grinning. "Critters'll come along an' enjoy all of this." She gathered the pencils and placed them in the pack, shaking her head and chuckling, seeming to enjoy a private joke. Finally she stood, reached for her drawing pad, and settled it against her hip. She turned to Jeremiah. "Let's head back." The teasing lilt still hovered in her voice.

Jeremiah struggled to his feet, embarrassed but greatly relieved to know he wouldn't be forced to consume comfrey leaves and stringy wild onions. But he liked this playful side of her. She seemed at ease with him and with herself, which pleased him immensely.

As soon as he settled his crutch beneath his left armpit, Tessy swung her head in the direction of the town, her brows coming down in alarm. She held up her hand. "Sh! Something's comin.'"

Had the food attracted a hungry bear? Jeremiah's heart thrummed as he waited, his ears alert and his eyes focused on the trees beyond the clearing.

"Tessy? Tessy McCleary? Are you out there?"

Tessy seemed to wilt for a moment, then she squared her shoulders and hollered, "I'm here! By the creek!"

A tall man emerged from the trees. His short-cropped hair was brushed severely back from his high forehead, revealing heavy brows which were pulled down into a scowl. He raised a large hand to shield his eyes. Jeremiah sensed the moment the man spotted the pair, because he came to a stop, and his hands lowered to rest on his hips in a stern stance.

"Tessy… Traipsing, as usual." The words held derision.

Shame slumped her shoulders. She bit down on her lower lip. Her fingers tightened on the drawing pad. "Hi, Pete."

10

Tessy waved good-bye to Jeremiah when they parted pathways behind the general store. She wished he would come to the house. She didn't want to be alone with her brother. Although Pete had involved Jeremiah in small-talk on the walk back to town, Tessy had seen his stiff bearing and heard the undercurrent of irritation in his tone.

Older than her by eleven years, Pete had never been a companion or playmate. Instead, he assumed a paternal role, becoming a second, less-than-loving father, quick to point out everything she did wrong. She embarrassed him, and while she longed for his approval, she remained uncertain how to gain it. Consequently she was always on edge around him.

They reached the house, and Pete opened the door, gesturing her inside. She scuttled to her bedroom to put away her drawing pad and pencils, but she didn't linger.

Pete would be waiting, and he wasn't a patient man. She spent a few precious seconds running a comb through her tangled hair and rubbing a wrinkled handkerchief over her shiny face in an attempt to make herself more presentable. A clean dress would be best, but she didn't want to squander more time. Another quick glance in the mirror, a grimace, then she headed toward the sitting area of the house.

As she passed the door to Mama and Pop's bedroom, she heard the quiet mumble of their voices. Had they deliberately shut themselves away to leave Pete and Tessy alone? Her anxiety increased. What did he want with her?

Pete waited at the kitchen table, his back to her, his spine straight and his head held at an arrogant angle. Tessy drew in a great breath of fortification before sitting across from him. He shook his head, disapproval evident in his gray eyes. "Tessy, when is this going to stop?"

Tessy scowled. "What?"

He slapped his hand onto the table top, and Tessy jumped. "The aimless wandering around the countryside. I saved up my gas rations to drive over from Searcy and spend time with the family, then I had to go trekking over the mountain to find you. You're too old for this nonsense. You're a woman, not a child. It's time to grow up."

Tessy cringed. "I—I don't know what you want me to do, Pete."

He sighed, raising his gaze to the overhead beams for a moment. He brought his hard gaze back to her and placed his interlocked fingers on the table top. "Ma and Pop told me what's been happening in town."

Everyone in town was concerned about the thefts, most of all her parents.

"I don't know if you're the one doing the stealing—"

His words cut her to the core. How could he not know? He was her brother. He should know she wasn't capable of such a horrible thing.

"—but if you are, it's got to stop right now. You can't make the people change their minds about you by engaging in something so inappropriate."

"Pete, I—"

He fixed her with a stern glare. "Listen to me. I've already talked to Ma and Pop, and they see the sense of what I'm about to suggest." He leaned forward while Tessy's heart pounded in sudden trepidation. "I believe you should move to Searcy."

Tessy gave a start. "You want me to move in with you?"

"We'll find you a job—perhaps in one of the shops in town or even some sort of janitorial position at the college. There are several boarding houses. I'm certain one of them would be willing to offer you a room."

Her heart fell. Of course he wouldn't want her with him.

"You'd have an opportunity to make a fresh start, to drop these odd behaviors and make some friends. Wouldn't you like that?"

"I don't know." Tessy shrugged. "You're thinkin' I should leave Shyler's Point for good?"

"Of course, leave Shyler's Point for good. What holds you here?" Pete threw out his arms in disgust. "You're the town scapegoat—an oddball, a misfit."

Tessy ducked her head, his words stinging like blows. She thought back to sitting beside the rock with Jeremiah. He had hugged her and told her she was a gift. Not a misfit, not an oddball—a gift. She let the words he uttered so sweetly while his blue eyes looked tenderly into hers soothe away the pain of Pete's harsh statement.

"Half the town has already left. The young men are off fighting, others have moved from the mountain to work in defense plants. The town is dying."

"Folks'll be back when the war is over."

Pete snorted. "You think those people are going to come back? There's nothing here to come back for. And even if they do return, how will that change anything? Tessy, you've never fit in here. From the time you were small, no one here has given you the time of day. Give me one good reason to stay in Shyler's Point."

Because Jeremiah Hatcher is here, an' he's gonna teach me to read. What would Pete say if she spoke the words aloud? She suspected Pete would call it a waste of time.

So she answered with the words that settled on her heart. "God ain't told me to go."

"'Ain't.'" Pete shook his head. "Listen to yourself. You sound like a hillbilly." He nearly spat the word, his eyes snapping. "That's what comes from hiding in those blasted hills all the time away from decent people. And if you think God is going to speak to you, you've been in the sun too long. God helps those who help themselves. Help yourself—take yourself away from here."

"But, Pete, I don't know nobody in Searcy, except you." Sadness sagged her shoulders. Once he secured a job for her and deposited her at the boarding house, she wouldn't see much of him. Pete wasn't trying to take her out of Shyler's Point to help her, but to ease his own humiliation for her role as town misfit.

"I didn't know anyone there, either, when I went. But I've made many friends, and I now look at Searcy as my home." He shifted in his chair, lifting his chin to peer down his nose at her. "Granted, my circle of friends is…older, and more sophisticated. I doubt you would feel comfortable spending time with them."

Tessy nodded. "'Course not."

"But I feel confident you would be able to find your own level of acceptance there. The community is larger and free from the ridiculous old-fashioned nonsense that makes everyone around here view you as an *ill wind*. Bah!" He waved a hand. "Tessy, there's another world outside of Shyler's Point. Take advantage of it. Move to Searcy."

She bit down on her lower lip. Going to Searcy would change nothing for her. She would still be an outcast, only this time it would be her own brother setting her aside. And now that she had formed a friendship with Jeremiah, she wanted to enjoy every minute possible with him, even if it would only be for a short amount of time. She hugged herself, already mourning his loss. "Ain't perfect, but Shyler's Point is home. I don't think I'm ready to leave it."

He stood and glared down at her. "If you want people to see you as an imbecile, keep talking like a simpleminded fool. Keep roaming around the countryside instead of holding a job and making something of yourself. Let those narrow-minded bigots continue to blame you for every misfortune that life throws their way. It's nothing to me!"

"Pete, it ain't—it isn't that I don't appreciate what you're offering," Tessy rose and stood timidly in front of him. "An' I want to believe you're doing it for my own good." He crossed his arms and turned his gaze away. She sighed. "But if I leave, it'll be the same as admitting guilt. An' I haven't done nothing wrong. I didn't take any of those things that've come up missing." He wouldn't look at her, and she hung her head. "It's gonna be pretty hard to make the town believe it if I can't even sway you…"

His fingers gripped her chin and brought her head up. He peered into her eyes, his brows lowered. "Are you telling me the truth, Tessy?"

"Yes."

He shoved his hands deep into his pockets. "Then that's all the more reason to get out of here. They've already tried and convicted you in their minds. They aren't going to change. There's no point in you staying here." He sighed, and his tone softened. "Think about what I said, Tessy. I'll be home for two more days. Think about coming to Searcy with me."

"All right."

His expression turned hard again. "If you say no, I won't ask again. Keep that in mind, too."

Tessy sank back down at the table as Pete headed through the passageway to the bedrooms. He was probably going in to tell Mama and Pop that he'd failed in convincing Tessy to leave. He'd probably also say how impossible she was, and how he regretted even making the offer. She sighed. A part of her considered doing as he suggested in the hopes of pleasing him. But would packing up and moving to Searcy bridge the gap between them? She doubted it. They'd be as far apart there as they had been here growing up in the same house.

She scraped the edge of the table with her thumbnail, scowling. Pete would be here for two more days. That meant no escapes to the mountains. And no seeing Jeremiah. She sat up straight, tears pricking her eyes. Jeremiah wouldn't be here long. She didn't have time to waste.

Her heart pounding, she rose and tiptoed to the passageway. She leaned forward, straining to hear. Yes, they were all still in there talking. Might be she'd have time to slip off for a bit before supper without being missed. Pete'd probably be mad if he came out and found her gone, but it was a chance she'd have to take. She needed to talk to Jeremiah.

"You sure the preacher is gonna be all right?"

Tessy froze next to the lilac bushes growing at the edge of the street outside the doc's house. She recognized Mrs. Spencer's strident tone, and the question puzzled her. Was Mrs. Spencer asking after Pop? She peeked around the corner, listening in while staying out of sight. The woman stood on the porch with the door to Doc Winters' office open, half in and half out.

Doc Winters' deep, male voice replied, but Tessy couldn't understand what he said.

"Sure scared me to see him tumble over like that. Never could decide what he caught his foot on. One minute he was up, talking with Flossie Pike in front o' the store, next minute he was lying on his belly in the dirt and she was screeching like a banshee. But if you're sure he's gonna be fine…"

Tessy's heart pounded so hard her ears thrummed, covering the sound. Tumbled over? It couldn't be Pop— Pop was at home in his bed. The only other preacher was Jeremiah. She covered her mouth with both hands to hold back any sound while her soul screamed in guilt and fear. She should've known. She should've known that being with Jeremiah would bring trouble to him.

"Well, now, you take care of yourself, Preacher. I'll look for you Wednesday evenin' at the Bible study." Mrs. Spencer's thick heels thudded on the porch boards, and Tessy ducked around to the other side of the lilacs to avoid being seen. She crouched amidst the leafy branches, waiting until the other woman was well down the path before emerging from her hiding spot.

Tessy turned her tear-filled eyes toward the heavens. "I didn't mean for something bad to happen. I just wanted to learn to read Your Word." The sun shone as brightly as before. No condemning lightning bolt came from above. But censure pressed upon her.

Twice she'd been with Jeremiah, and twice the ill wind had touched him. First just a splash of soda, but this time... How bad was he hurt? She closed her eyes, picturing him pitching forward into the dirt. Lying there hurt, bleeding, broken... She wouldn't be able to fix this with a scrub board and soap. Tears coursed down her cheeks.

"I'm so sorry, Jeremiah," she whispered. "I won't hurt

you again. I'll leave Shyler's Point before I let anything else happen to you." She'd told Pete that God hadn't directed her to leave Shyler's Point, but maybe this was His way of forcing her out of town.

It would break her heart to leave, but she'd rather cut off her own arm than hurt Jeremiah after his kindness to her. She wiped away her tears and swallowed the lump of sorrow filling her dry throat. "It won't happen again, Jeremiah, I promise…" Then she scurried back down the path to her own house to find her brother and give him her decision.

11

Jeremiah lay on the examination table while Holden cleaned and bandaged his scraped palms and chin. "It's been a long time since I've done something like this. At least in the light of day. I set my crutch wrong on the ground and it tripped me." He shook his head ruefully. "That poor woman—what was her name? Flossie Tate? I'll have to apologize to her. I think I nearly gave her apoplexy."

"Oh, Flossie's a tough old bird. She'll recover." Holden wrapped strips of gauze around Jeremiah's left hand. "It'll give her something exciting to share with the Ladies Missionary Society when they get together to roll bandages on Thursday."

"I can hear it." Jeremiah changed his tone to emulate an older woman's warble. "'Fell at my feet, he did. Just up an' fell at my feet...'"

Holden grinned wickedly. "Flossie is almost eight-five years old. At her age, it's a treat to have a man fall at her feet. And speaking of feet, let's get you up on yours. I don't think you did any damage below your waist."

Jeremiah let Holden pull him into a seated position. Then he pushed himself upright, wincing as his scraped palms rested on the table. He stood unsteadily until Holden gave him his crutch. With his crutch under his arm, he felt more secure. He wasn't in a great deal of pain, just a bit shaken from his unexpected spill. "I hope I didn't break my braces. These scuffs on my hand will heal fine. Metal isn't so easily fixed."

Holden bent down on one knee and carefully examined the braces. "I see a couple of scratches on the right one, but no dents. They look okay to me, Jeremiah." Then he frowned. "Hold still a minute."

Jeremiah waited while Holden plucked something from between his braces and his pant leg.

"I thought you fell in the street."

"I did."

"Then where did this come from?" Holden held up a small clump of moss and part of a leaf. "These were caught in your braces. Neither would be found growing in the street."

Jeremiah grinned. He must have picked those up when he sat on the river bank with Tessy. He thought of her enthusiastic response to his Bible reading and her impish grin while trying to convince him to eat comfrey leaves. "My woods picnic."

"Woods picnic?" Holden gave him an odd look. "Maybe I should check you for head injuries."

Jeremiah laughed. "My head is fine." Then he sighed. "However, my heart might be in trouble."

"Oh?" Holden crossed his arms. "Why is that?"

Jeremiah sighed, shifting to rest his hips against the table. "May I ask you a personal question?"

"Sure."

"How long did it take for you to know that you loved Callie?"

Holden's eyebrows shot up. "Have you found love on our mountain, Jeremiah?"

Jeremiah rubbed his nose, chuckling. "Could be. But I've only just met her. How quickly can love grow?"

Holden shoved his hands into his pockets, sending a smirk in Jeremiah's direction. "You know, it's funny. I had a similar conversation with your brother Micah several years ago. He thought he was falling in love with Callie, and I questioned how it could happen so quickly. Yet, what he felt was very real." He paused, chewing the inside of his cheek. "I think love strikes in a variety of ways. Sometimes it grows slowly and steadily, without you even realizing it's happening, until you wake up one morning and know that life isn't complete without the other person by your side. That's how it was with Callie— an interest that took on a life of its own despite my best efforts to hold it back.

"Other times it hits like a waterfall, takes your breath away, sends you tumbling head over heels, and leaves you wondering if your feet will ever touch the ground again. With my first wife I got hit by the waterfall. Maybe because I was younger and the young tend to be more dramatic."

Jeremiah remembered Micah speaking of Holden's first wife and the infant son who were killed in a fire many years ago. But Holden had found the ability to love again, and soon he would have another chance for fatherhood. "I can't say I've been hit by a waterfall, but what I'm experiencing isn't exactly a slow growth, either." He huffed. "So how can I know for sure?"

Callie stepped through the doorway, her expression innocent. "Know what?"

Holden glanced at Jeremiah, as if seeking permission to share the topic. Jeremiah gave a one shoulder shrug then nodded. Holden asked, "How can a person know for sure if he's falling in love?"

Callie fit herself snugly against Holden's side. "Easy. When your days and nights are haunted by the face and voice of another person, when you feel as if you can't make it through the day unless you can see that face or hear that voice close by, when making that person happy becomes more important than pleasing yourself, then you know you're in love." She peered up at Holden.

"Why? Who's falling in love?"

"Maybe no one," Jeremiah said, "but I need some guidance, and I would greatly appreciate it if you two would pray for me. What I might be feeling is simply Christian caring for a fellow human being, but it sure felt like more this morning when I held her in my arms."

"What?" Callie's green eyes flew wide.

Jeremiah's ears turned hot. "It was just a little spontaneous hug. Nothing to get all excited about." Then he chuckled. "Of course, maybe it was enough to get me sufficiently off kilter to fall face first into the dirt..." He held up his bandaged hands and smirked.

Callie's face pinched in sympathy as she cupped her belly with both hands. "Oh, that must have hurt. You're probably hungry, too, since you weren't here for lunch. I left a plate on the back of the stove for you. It should still be warm, if you want to go eat."

"That sounds good." Jeremiah led with his crutch and stepped away from the table. "I think I will go have a bite."

Holden gave Callie a quick kiss on the forehead and set her aside. "And I'll get things cleaned up in here."

She moved to the doorway. "And I'll go to my bedroom and get comfortable, because the way I figure it, I'm going to be a mother before morning." She gave a mischievous grin and flipped her hands outward, as if to say *surprise!*, then left the room without a backward glance.

Jeremiah froze.

Holden's head whipped toward the doorway.

Both men stared at each other stupidly for a few stunned seconds.

Jeremiah cleared his throat. "Did she just say what I think she just said?"

Holden nodded, the movement jerky. "Yes." His face took on an expression of wonder. "Which means I'll be a father by morning…" He shook his head, his brow furrowing with worry. "But the baby isn't due for another two weeks." He dashed out the door.

Jeremiah followed in his slow gait. Callie's calm voice carried up the hallway.

"Now, you know a due date isn't carved in stone. Babies can come anytime within two weeks of that date, whether before or after."

Jeremiah peeked into the room. Holden sat on the edge of the bed and held Callie's hand. "Yes, but first babies are notoriously late."

Callie chuckled, her belly bouncing. "Apparently no one explained that to our baby. Believe me, this baby is ready to make its appearance, and I would prefer that its first sight wasn't your fear-filled face. Will you relax?" She reached up and touched his cheek. "Holden, please, I've never done this before. I'm going to need you to pull yourself together."

Holden dropped his head to her hand, pressing her

knuckles against his forehead for a moment. Then he kissed the knuckles and gently placed her hand on the bed. He stood and leaned over her, bestowing a lingering kiss on her lips. Jeremiah continued to watch from the doorway, feeling like an intruder yet unable to turn away.

"How far apart are the contractions?" Holden sounded brisk and businesslike now.

"Between five and six minutes. They started a little over three hours ago."

"Okay." Holden gave her another quick kiss then straightened. "I'm going after your aunts. They'll want to be here. I won't be gone long. You rest. There will be time to get everything ready when I get back."

Callie smiled. "I'm fine, Holden. Go ahead."

Holden started to leave, then returned to the bed to kiss her again. "I love you." His voice sounded thick with tears.

"I know. I love you, too."

Holden rushed past Jeremiah and headed straight down the hallway to the parlor. The front door slammed.

Jeremiah peered in at Callie who lay quietly, her ankles crossed and her hands resting on her round stomach. "Can—" His voice cracked. He cleared his throat and tried again. "Can I get anything for you?"

Callie rolled her head sideways to smile at him. "No, I'm fine. Go eat your lunch." She waved at him.

Jeremiah backed away from the door and clumped

his way to the kitchen. It hurt to grasp the handhold on his crutch, but he ignored the pain, his thoughts on Callie and Holden. How would he feel if it were his wife preparing to bring forth his child? He couldn't imagine.

He removed the checked napkin covering the plate on the back of the stove then carried the plate of chicken and dumplings to the table. He sat and folded his hands in prayer.

God, be with Callie and the little one who's preparing to come into the world. Keep them both safe. Be with Holden as he helps his child be born. He paused, his heart pattering. *And, Lord, if You see fit, allow me the opportunity to become a husband and father someday, to experience the joy that Callie and Holden are preparing to enjoy now.*

Behind his closed eyelids, Tessy's sweet face appeared, her eyes shining, her hair blowing gently across her cheeks.

If it's love, God, and it's Your will, help it flourish for both of us.

Jeremiah glanced at the clock above the mantel and winced. Almost two in the morning. If he was tired of waiting, he could only imagine how Callie and Holden felt. Callie's white-haired aunts were nearly nodding off right there on the sofa.

"Would you ladies like to lie down?" The pair sat up

like two chipmunks popping out of a hole in the ground, their eyes flying wide. He hid a smile. "You're welcome to use the bed I've been sleeping in."

"Oh, no, we'll stay awake until we hear the baby's cry," Vivian said.

Viola nodded. "There will be time for sleeping later, when we know everything is well."

Jeremiah shifted into the corner of the chair and bowed his head in prayer once more. Sleep tugged hard, and he began to drift off, but an odd noise intruded. He jerked upright. Both of the aunts were scurrying down the hallway. Realization struck—the mewling noise was a baby's cry.

He snapped the locks on his braces with shaky hands and pushed himself to his feet. Grabbing his crutch, he followed the two older ladies as quickly as he could. The bedroom door flew open from the inside, and Holden stood in the doorway with a smile lighting his face and tears glittering in his eyes.

"We have a girl!" He hugged first Vivian and then Viola. "Evangelina Rose Winters, born at two-forty-two in the morning on July 15, 1945. I haven't weighed her yet, but I don't think she'll be much more than six pounds. She's a tiny mite, but scrappy. Listen to that wail!"

The infant's boisterous complaints flowed into the hallway.

Vivian clasped her hands beneath her chin. "Can we see her?"

Viola tried to peer past Holden's shoulder.

Holden gestured for them to enter. "Come on in. Just look at her! Isn't she a beauty?"

Jeremiah clumped in behind the aunts who separated to lean over opposite sides of the bed. They stroked Callie's hair and cooed over the tiny girl cradled in a rumpled blanket in Callie's arms. Jeremiah remained at the end of the bed where Holden stood beside him.

Holden's chest puffed and his face glowed. "Just look at my beautiful baby girl."

Jeremiah looked at the baby's smashed nose, swollen eyes, and wrinkled face. He remembered peeking into a robin's nest as a boy. The baby girl's pink, wrinkled skin and funny tufts of hair were similar to the featherless robin babies. He shook his head, smiling to himself. Beauty was most certainly in the eye of the beholder. He gave Holden's shoulder a hearty clap. "Congratulations, Holden. You, too, Callie."

Callie offered a weary smile. The little girl found her fist and sucked noisily. The three women laughed softly. Callie looked at Holden. "Should I try to nurse her?"

"Yes. We'll all clear out and let you two have some time alone."

"Oh, no," Viola said. "You should stay, Daddy."

"Daddy..." Fresh tears appeared in Holden's eyes. He stepped to the edge of the bed and touched the baby's fuzzy head, seeming to forget about everyone else in the room.

The aunts ushered Jeremiah out the door and to the parlor. There, they sank down side by side on the sofa and smiled.

Vivian released a sigh. "Another generation is born."

Viola looked up at Jeremiah. "Preacher, would you say a prayer of thanks for the new little life that's just entered the world?"

"Certainly." Jeremiah stepped close and they joined hands. "Heavenly Father, thank You for the safe arrival of Evangelina Rose. May this little soul learn early to look to You for guidance. May her parents always seek You for knowledge and wisdom to train her in the way she should go. We praise Your name for the precious gift that has been given to Callie and Holden. Keep them safe in Your precious arms. In Your name we pray, amen."

"Amen," both ladies echoed.

Viola yawned. "Now I can sleep."

"Me, too." Vivian stood. "Jeremiah, could we possibly trouble you to escort us home?"

"Now?" He wasn't keen on marching across the uneven pathways in the dark after falling on one of them during daylight hours. "Can't you sleep here?"

"I need my own bed. And I'm sure the children would prefer not to have us underfoot during these first precious hours with their new baby." She pursed her lips and tapped them with one finger. "In fact, young man, you could stay at the house and sleep there, if you'd like. Then if the baby cries, you won't be disturbed."

Jeremiah considered the offer. Sometimes he felt like an interloper. Maybe it would be a good idea to allow Callie and Holden this time alone. Besides, Vivian's house was only a bit beyond the McCleary dogtrot. In the morning he could visit Tessy. "Thank you for the invitation, ladies. Let me find a lantern, and then we'll head out."

12

A strange of sense of *déjà vu* gripped Jeremiah as he walked behind Viola's swinging lantern with Vivian holding tightly to his elbow. The lantern's mild movement created odd shadows that gave the illusion of specters dancing amidst the bushes and trees. He found himself listening for soldiers or hostile civilians while his heart pounded in worry. Why couldn't he remember he was with two sweet ladies in Shyler's Point, Arkansas, not in the Polish countryside with exiled Jews?

He forced his attention to their surroundings. The moon hung heavy overhead, seeming to play hide and seek with wispy clouds that drifted across the night sky. From a tree nearby, a hoot owl called in a low-pitched query, and a second one answered in soprano. The breeze carried sweet scents of burgeoning fall. Jeremiah inhaled deeply to fully enjoy the pleasant smells.

Viola stopped and turned, bringing Jeremiah and

Vivian into a halo of light. "Shall we cut through the Mc-Cleary's back yard? It will shorten our distance."

Vivian yawned. "That's a good idea. I'm ready to tumble into my bed."

Viola angled her steps toward the back of the minister's dogtrot.

As they crossed the yard, Jeremiah remembered coming back here on wash day. Tessy's sweaty face and spattered dress front filled his memory. How could she look so pretty even when rumpled? Memories of Poland slipped further away.

The trio rounded the back corner of the house, and Jeremiah noticed the yellow glow of a lantern's flame behind a curtain-shrouded window. "Someone must be up."

Vivian gave a slight shrug. "Oh, I'm sure she's sleeping. She leaves the lantern on all night."

Jeremiah frowned. "She?"

"Tessy." Vivian's fingers tightened on Jeremiah's arm. "From the time she was a little girl, the lantern has burned all night." She lowered her voice, assuming a secretive air. "On the nights the light has gone out, the sounds have been terrible—cries of complete terror." She shook her head. "She's very frightened of the dark."

Jeremiah's heart turned over in sympathy. Had something happened to her to create this fear? Many Jewish people were afraid of the dark for good reason. Often the SS men came to wreak their havoc after the lights fell low.

But what had developed this fear in Tessy?

Another thought struck him. "Then how can the townspeople believe Tessy is the one stealing from them? If she's afraid of the dark, she certainly isn't out at night, looking for things to take, is she?"

Vivian shot him a quick look, her brows furrowed. "Most times the things have disappeared during the light of day. Rarely at night." She sighed again. "Which of course helps to point the finger of blame at Tessy."

A band seemed to constrict his chest. "Do you think Tessy is the one stealing?"

Viola turned quickly, the lantern swinging wildly and making the shadows perform a war dance. "Of course not! Neither of us believe that nonsense. Tessy is a sweet girl who would never bring harm to anyone. Why, when she was little, she brought us wildflower bouquets." She huffed, a hand on her bulky hip. "Some folks around town liked to poke the finger of fun at my sister and me because we were unmarried, but that little girl brought us flowers. There's not a mean bone in her body, and it angers me to no end that these superstitious ding-dongs insist she's an *ill wind*. Ha!" Viola squared her shoulders and lifted her knobby chin. "They don't mention such nonsense to my face without getting an earful in return, I can tell you that!"

Jeremiah's heart warmed toward this crusty woman. "You are a dear lady, Miss Viola."

Viola tittered, touching the ruffled bodice of her dress with a vein-lined hand. "And you are a true gentleman, Preacher Hatcher." She blushed, then spun on her heel and advanced to the little clapboard house just ahead.

Jeremiah and Vivian followed without speaking. Shortly both women were snoring in their beds, and Jeremiah was stretched out on the sofa in the small parlor, a patchwork quilt thrown across his legs. Though tired and longing to sleep, his mind refused to shut down. He lay, hands beneath his head, staring at the plaster ceiling, while an image of Tessy's glowing bedroom window burned in his memory.

The soft mumble of voices outside her window had brought Tessy awake and instantly fearful. But a peek out her window settled her racing pulse. She needn't fear Jeremiah and the Myers sisters. They'd closed themselves in their house minutes ago, but she still gazed across the dark yard, recalling Jeremiah's slow but steady progress. Such a relief to see him walking. After overhearing Mrs. Spencer's comments, she'd feared he might be unable to walk.

And, she had to admit, more than relief, it was a pleasure to see him.

She dropped the curtain and sank down on the edge

of her mattress. The corn husks crackled with her weight, and she flopped backward, creating a louder rustle. She covered her eyes with her arm and fought the sting of tears. He'd been so good to her. Her feelings for him went clear down deep in her soul. She wished she was different, better, so she could be deserving of him. But wishing never changed anything. It was best she'd be leaving. He'd be safer. The thought made her stomach ache.

Maybe if Pete's response to her decision had been more positive, Tessy could be at peace. When she told him she would go to Searcy, he had scowled, giving her the superior look she knew well, and huffed, "Well, I'm surprised. You made a sensible choice." And then he'd turned to Pop and began speaking of other things, as if Tessy wasn't planning to turn her whole world upside-down.

She allowed her gaze to rove around the room, examining—almost memorizing—every small detail from the rough-hewn walls pinned with pictures of animals saved from calendars to the simple furnishings that had belonged to Mama's mother and ending with the burning lantern beside her bed. There'd be electricity in the boarding house at Searcy. She'd need to purchase one of those lamps with the cord that plugged in to keep beside her bed. No more coal oil. That might be nice.

But maybe, in Searcy, the shadows wouldn't be so deep. Maybe she wouldn't feel the need to keep a light burning through the darkness to dispel the shadows…

"They that dwell in the land o' the shadder o' death, upon them hath the light shined…"

Ol' Gordy's words drifted through Tessy's memory once more. Where'd he gotten those words? Didn't seem like something he'd come up with himself. He must've heard them somewhere. Or read them. She'd like to find the light that shined on the land of the shadow of death. She figured it would be bright enough to chase away her shadows for good.

She whispered to the quiet room, "I want to live without fear."

There was so much Tessy wanted to know. When Jeremiah had read from the Bible to her—page after page of words and phrases—her heart had thrilled, thinking that soon she'd be able to pick up the Book and read the words for herself. She sensed freedom from fear was caught in the pages of God's Book, and she wanted to find it with her own eyes, read it aloud with her own voice.

She punched her mattress in aggravation. She wanted to learn to read. Jeremiah wanted to teach her. Would someone in Searcy teach her? She rolled onto her stomach and buried her face in the crumpled quilt, allowing the tears pressing behind her lids to burst their dam and flow freely.

"I'll just be takin' the fear with me." The folds of fabric muffled her voice. "It'll never leave me be…"

Jeremiah awakened just before seven. He lay, listening to the clock on the mantel chime, and at the final chord he struggled into his braces. His muscles were stiff, partly from sleeping on the hard cushions, but mostly from his tumble in the dirt yesterday. A series of bruises ran up and down both shins, but he was thankful he hadn't seriously hurt himself. Releasing a slight groan, he rose and forced his hips into motion.

The house was completely silent other than the ticking of the clock. A note on the kitchen table indicated the aunts had taken breakfast to Callie and Holden—he would find biscuits and bacon in the hob of the stove and should help himself. The food was still warm, and he ate leisurely, enjoying the quiet of the morning. He rinsed his plate and placed it in the sink with the other dishes, then headed to the little dogtrot below the aunts' house, anxious to share news of Evangelina's birth with the Mc-Cleary's.

Mrs. McCleary answered his knock and greeted him with a huge smile. "Why, good morning, Preacher! Isn't it wonderful that Doc and Callie's little girl has arrived? Fit and healthy, and pretty as a rose bush, from the way it's been told."

Jeremiah swallowed a chortle. Who was telling the story? No one who'd gotten a good long look at the wrinkled little bundle named Evangelina Rose.

The woman wiped her hands on her apron. "I don't figure Callie is up to puttering in her kitchen, so Tessy and I are baking an extra cinnamon cake to take over there. Come on in and have a piece with us."

He should mention that Callie's aunts had already seen to breakfast, but a whiff of a delightful aroma changed his mind. Despite the fact that he'd just eaten, his stomach seemed to sit up and beg. An extra cinnamon cake would be welcome. Besides, Tessy bustled around at the back of the room, her shining hair beckoning to him.

He smiled and stepped over the threshold. "Thank you, Mrs. McCleary. I appreciate the invitation." He sat at the table with Tessy's somber brother.

Tessy placed a sizable wedge of crumbly cake in front of him and then disappeared through the breezeway. Jeremiah ate his cake with Mrs. McCleary and Pete. The moist, cinnamon-laden cake was delicious, but he had a hard time swallowing. Why had Tessy run off? He thought she'd gotten beyond her need to hide. At least from him.

His glanced at the tall man across the table. For an intelligent man, Pete McCleary wasn't much for conversation. Pete ate in silence, his left hand in his lap. Although Mrs. McCleary broke off bite-sized chunks of cake with her fingers, Pete used a fork to cut off small pieces of the cake and carry it to his mouth. He used his napkin often, sipped his coffee without a sound. For reasons he didn't understand Jeremiah found the man's impeccable manners annoying. He was relieved when breakfast was finished and he could excuse himself.

"Thank you again, Mrs. McCleary. That was delicious. Would you please let Tessy know I'll be by mid-morning?"

Pete paused with the coffee cup beneath his chin. "Why?"

Jeremiah had been addressing Mrs. McCleary and didn't want to answer Pete's abrupt question, but he'd been taught to be polite. "She and I are working on a project. I want to check its progress."

"I can't imagine what kind of project Tessy would have with a minister." Pete took a sip of coffee. "Tessy might be busy today. She is packing to accompany me to Searcy."

Had Jeremiah received the news with a bite in his mouth, he probably would have spewed the contents across the table, so great was his surprise. "You mean packing things for you to take into Searcy?"

Pete frowned. "No. Packing her own items. She's moving to Searcy and taking a job in the city."

Jeremiah reeled. Why would she do this after being so enthusiastic about learning to read? Something was terribly amiss. He looked from Pete's impassive face to Mrs. McCleary's closed expression. He'd get no answers here.

He'd have to wait and talk to Tessy. If she would see him.

He moved slowly toward the front door. "Please give Tessy the message. I'm sure she'll be able to take a small break from her packing to visit with me."

Pete gave another shrug, as if it was no concern of his. "We'll let her know. Tell the Winters congratulations for me. Have a good day, Preacher."

The dismissal irritated Jeremiah, but he managed a stiff smile and good-bye. Out under the bright morning sun, he aimed his crutch toward the Winters' home. Mrs. McCleary had said the baby was as pretty as a rose bush. He'd go check that out for himself, see how the little one must have changed in the past few hours, and do what he could to be helpful to the new parents. Bide his time and wait for mid-morning to arrive. And then he would knock again on the McCleary cabin door, but this time he wouldn't allow Tessy to sneak away. This time he would find out why she was running. He hoped she wasn't running from him.

13

Jeremiah never learned how it happened. Few people in Shyler's Point had telephone service in their homes. The sun had barely cleared the horizon. The baby was less than eight hours old. Yet the whole town seemed to be abuzz with news of the latest member of the Winters' family.

On his trek across the tiny community to the Winters' home, he was stopped no less than seven times, and each person raved about the new addition. As Jeremiah clumped his way up the porch steps, he heard a flurry of female voices and Holden's tired baritone. Holden would probably be relieved to see a male face.

He knocked on the screen door, but no one answered, so he entered. The hubbub came from the direction of the kitchen. He moved toward the small room at the back of the house. Glancing down the hallway, he noticed Callie's bedroom door was closed. He swallowed a smirk. Smart girl, leaving Holden to deal with the masses.

Comments and Holden's replies drifted from the kitchen.

"Now, Doc, aren't you the lucky one. A girl child first! She'll be such a help to her mama."

"Yes, I'm certain she—"

"Such a pretty name, too. Evangelina. Will you call her Evvie? Or Vangie? Or Lina? Oh, my, you can do so much with that name, can't you?"

"Well, we'll probably just call her—"

"Mighty small, isn't she? Reckon you've got plenty of ways of pertin' her up. When my baby brother was born small an' sickly, my mama fed him ground calf liver and cream. Just built him up good. But use raw liver—if you cook it, takes all the iron right out of it."

"To be honest, I doubt that—"

"Aw, girls don't need to be all built up, Maggie. That baby's just gonna be dainty, like her mama."

"Now, I tend to agree with—"

"And a Tuesday's child, full of grace…"

Jeremiah shook his head. Little wonder Callie closed the door on all that. Instead of going into the kitchen and being exposed to more of the ladies' wisdom, he clumped back out to the porch and settled himself on the swing. A movement beside the gate caught his attention. He swung his gaze, and his heart expanded. Tessy stood on the opposite side, a covered plate in her hands.

He smiled and waved. "Good morning! Is that the cinnamon cake for Callie and Holden? Bring it on in."

But she stayed on the other side of the gate, unsmiling.

A shiver of foreboding attacked as he remembered her hasty exit this morning. Had he done something to offend her? He stood. "Is everything all right?"

"I'll just leave this here." She pushed the gate open and placed the plate on the stepping stone inside the fence. "Will you tell Doc an' Callie that Mama sends her warmest regards? With Pete visitin', she didn't feel she could get away herself."

What had happened to the smiling young woman who teased him about not eating her woods picnic only yesterday? Where was the enthusiasm about learning to read God's Word? Jeremiah felt as if he'd lost his last friend. Tessy turned to leave, and panic rose in his chest.

"Wait!"

She paused, her gaze still angled away from him. Her shoulders seemed stiff, her body tense.

He thumped down the steps at a reckless pace and hobbled across the stepping stones. But he stopped on his side of the gate. "Have I done something to offend you? If so, I'm terribly sorry."

She didn't answer, but the muscles in her back quivered. Was she crying?

"Your brother said you were packing to accompany

him to Searcy. Is that true? Are you leaving?"

She nodded. One quick bob of her head.

"Why? Is it—is it because of me?" He held his breath.

A dreadful pause followed while her body quivered and he silently prayed.

"Yes."

One word, uttered low and in a painfully thin voice. She shot him an anguished look, a fist raised to her lips, then she raced up the street, her bare feet slapping the ground hard.

Jeremiah remained at the gate, holding onto the pickets with shaking hands, tears stinging his nose, until she rounded the curve behind the general store and disappeared from view.

Tessy hoped her mama and brother would assume she'd stayed to chat with Doc. With all the packing she had to do, there wasn't time to be running to the woods, but she needed to escape. She couldn't go home with tears on her cheeks, not without facing questions she didn't want to answer. So she ran behind the general store, over the rise, and across the brief expanse of meadow. She didn't slow down until she was well into the stand of maples beyond.

Safe within the shelter of trees, she dropped to her knees on a bed of moss and leaves, clutched her belly with both arms, and allowed the tears to flow. Noisy tears. Harsh tears. Tears which frightened the birds into flight from the red and gold decorated branches overhead.

"I'm sorry, I'm sorry." She didn't know who the apology was to. To Jeremiah for getting hurt, to herself for being too weak to stand up to her brother, or to God for always doing the wrong thing.

Jeremiah had asked if she was leaving because of him. She'd told the truth. She was leaving because of him. But not because he'd done anything wrong. He'd done everything right. But she was a danger to him. She couldn't stay and let him be hurt anymore. Yet she sensed her answer had hurt him, and it pained her deeply to know that even in her attempts to protect him, she was causing him distress. But what other choice did she have? She couldn't allow her ill wind to touch him again. If she stayed, it would certainly happen again, and maybe next time it would be worse. Her brother's offer to take her to Searcy had to be God's way of protecting Jeremiah.

Her wild crying finally came to an end. She wiped the moisture from her cheeks, settled back against the trunk of the sturdy maple, and closed her eyes. Going was the right thing. Pete thought so, and Mama and Pop agreed. At least they hadn't argued. The town wouldn't miss her. Jeremiah might, and she'd miss him. She'd miss the friendship he offered. She'd miss the chance to learn. But she couldn't be selfish. She had to keep him safe. Her chest ached so bad it hurt to breathe. She needed comforting.

Suddenly part of sermon her father had given when she was still a little girl tiptoed through her mind. She whispered, her brow furrowed in concentration, "Went somethin' like fear not, 'cause God is with you. He'll help and uphold you…"

Tipping up her chin, she opened her eyes and spoke to the blue sky peeking between the branches of the massive trees. "God, I need upholdin' now. I'm scared that somehow I'm gonna hurt Jeremiah. Hold me up, keep my ill wind from touchin' him again. Help me, God, please…"

She sat, listening to the breeze move through the branches. Two cardinals—a brightly colored male and his plain mate—returned to sing a cheerful melody. Gentle came from the creek—maybe the beavers hard at work, or frisky trout leaping into the sunshine. In time her spirit calmed, and she was ready to face her family.

As she rose and brushed off the seat of her skirt, she murmured, "Not sure what I'm gonna say to Pete when I get home. Not sure if I'm goin' or stayin'. But, God, I'm trustin' You to give me the words that are right and the strength to say 'em. Amen."

Jeremiah hadn't been able to open the door with Tessy's plate in his hand, so he waited on the porch swing for someone to come along and take the cake inside. Nearly twenty minutes passed before Holden stepped out on the porch, his brow furrowed and his lips set in a grim line.

He plopped onto the swing next to Jeremiah and pointed to the cake. "What's this?"

"Cinnamon cake from Mrs. McCleary. Tessy brought it by."

"She didn't want to come in and see the baby?"

Jeremiah raised his eyebrows. The cacophony continued from inside, and Holden gave a rueful grimace. Tessy wouldn't have been welcome in their midst, so why stay?

Holden took the cake. "Do you want to come in?"

"No, thanks. It's peaceful out here."

Holden nodded, sighed, and went back inside the house.

Jeremiah listened to the flutter of voices. One of the women had recited part of a poem when talking about the baby, branding little Evangelina "full of grace" for having been born on Tuesday. If he recalled the poem correctly, Friday's child—which would be Tessy—was loving and giving. While he put no stock in such things determining a child's personality, the description seemed to fit. Even though Tessy had said she was leaving because of him, even though she had run away, he suspected there was something else at the heart of this change. Something that had more to do with Tessy and the town than himself.

He released a snort. Or maybe he was just trying to convince himself. Although it seemed logical she would want to leave Shyler's Point after the town's mistreatment of her, maybe his appearance—his unwanted attention—had finally given her the impetus needed to force her off the mountain. He'd never been cynical as a youth, but he had changed in the past few years.

The Jeremiah who overcame polio and learned to walk again, who completed the schooling to become an ordained minister, who crossed the ocean during the height of war and reached out to people of a completely different faith no longer existed. He had been beaten down by the war, scarred by his failure to save more people from Hitler's rampages, and he didn't have the strength to fight anything else. Why set himself up for failure again?

Maybe Tessy's leaving was for the best. He wasn't a teacher. He had no business offering to teach Tessy to read. It was doomed to fail. She was better off in Searcy with her brother who could find her a real teacher. She could find friends—people who weren't afraid to spend time with her out of some misplaced superstitious nonsense. She'd be happy there.

Moving to Searcy was best for Tessy. Best for him. He told himself that over and over. Yet his heart remained unconvinced.

14

According to Holden, Wednesday evening Bible study was a casual time of Bible reading, singing, and fellowship, so Jeremiah placed a stool on the raised floor at the front of the chapel. He sat and draped his Bible across his thighs. "Please open your Bibles to the fourth chapter of Matthew."

Tessy sat in her familiar pew with her head low, and Pete sat behind her. She gripped a Bible, but Pete's hands were empty. Was he the kind of man who relied on his own intelligence and strength to make it through the days?

Jeremiah pulled his attention away from Tessy and her brother. "Would someone read the first eleven verses for us?"

Silence fell. People exchanged confused glances. Finally a man in faded overalls and a plaid shirt rose from a middle pew and gave a self-conscious shrug. "Reckon I can do it, Preacher."

"Thank you. Go ahead."

The man read straight through, using a monotone voice and occasionally stumbling over words, but he made it to the end. The moment he finished, he plunked his behind on the bench and heaved a sigh.

Jeremiah flashed a smile in the man's direction. "There are two things I want us to consider in this section. First of all, Jesus was tempted. The Son of God in human form was tempted by the greatest tempter of all. At the time, Jesus was hungry and tired. It would have been so much simpler to give in to what Satan asked of Him, to turn rocks into bread and satisfy his hunger, to give in to the devil and accept all that he offered. But what did Jesus do instead?"

He paused, waiting for an answer from the floor. People stared at him as if dumbstruck. After an interminable time of silence, a reedy voice spoke from the front pew.

"He…He resisted?"

Jeremiah swung his gaze in that direction, battling against a cry of exultation. "That's right. He resisted. And what did Satan do?"

Tessy swallowed, obviously aware that every face in the room was turned toward her. He prayed she'd find the courage to answer.

"He left."

Jeremiah nodded. "That's right. In the light of Jesus'

resistance, Satan had no choice but to leave. James 4:7 tells us that if we resist the devil, he will flee. If the devil has a foothold in our lives, the finger of blame can only be aimed in one direction."

He flipped a page in his Bible. "Let's drop down a few verses." He wanted to give Tessy extra attention—to rest his gaze on her pale face and coax a smile out of her. But he turned his attention to his Bible and began to read. He came to verse sixteen and enunciated each word carefully. "'The people which sat in darkness saw great light; and to them which sat in the region and shadow of death light is sprung up.'"

Tessy gasped, but he determinedly kept from turning in her direction. "We could exchange the word 'light' with a name. What name would that be?"

This time several voices chimed in. "Jesus."

"Yes. Jesus." Jeremiah spoke as much to himself as to the people gathered in the simple sanctuary. "Jesus is the Light that shines through every darkness, the Light that dispels every shadow. And until we find Him, until we form a personal relationship with Him, where are we walking?"

A slight pause followed, then the same man who had offered to read earlier hesitantly answered. "In the shadow of death?"

Jeremiah nodded eagerly. "That's right. Without Jesus, we are headed for eternal darkness, separated from the love of God. But with Jesus, we have the light that breaks through every darkness, even the darkness of the shadow of death. We have the opportunity for eternal life in His presence."

Tears pricked his eyes, and his throat caught. A desire to experience the light of God's presence welled up in his aching soul and he closed his eyes, fighting the dark memories of sneaking through the night, heart pounding, fear quivering through his belly. *Remove those shadows from my soul, Lord, please.*

He opened his eyes and blinked to clear the moisture. "Jesus came to be the light that floods every darkness. Jesus came to help us resist the temptations of the world. When we walk in His presence, then we truly are walking in the light, well above the shadowy valleys that fill us with fear and doubt." He held up his Bible and recited again, "'The people which sat in darkness saw great light; and to them which sat in the region and shadow of death light is sprung up.'

"These words were written in the Old Testament for a group of people who lived long before Jesus came into the world in human form. They were recorded so those people would watch for the Light. Then, in the New Testament, they're repeated so the people to whom Jesus spoke could know that now the Light was among them." He leaned forward slightly, resting one hand on a knee while holding up his worn Bible with his other hand.

"These words apply to us today. If you're walking without Jesus, you're in the shadow of death. Reach out to Him. Reach out for His light, let it spring up in your soul, and walk in the Light of God."

Tessy listened, her thoughts jumbled. He'd said her verse—the verse that had plagued her thoughts. How had he known? Realization struck, causing her heart to patter in wild abandon. Jeremiah spoke the words God placed on his heart. God knew what she needed to hear.

Jeremiah straightened, closed his Bible, and smiled gently at the congregation. He turned to Doc Winters, who sat on the opposite side of the church on the front pew. "Come lead us in a closing hymn, Holden. I suggest 'In the Garden.'"

Voices around her lifted in song, but Tessy sat silently with a lump of emotion blocking her throat.

"...And He walks with me, and He talks with me; and He tells me I am His own..."

Wasn't that why Tessy escaped to the mountains? To walk with Jesus and hear His voice? She heard His voice now as the music swelled softly throughout the sanctuary. Going to Searcy might be what Pete wanted. It might even be what Tessy wanted, just to protect Jeremiah from harm. But it wasn't what God wanted. There was something she needed to finish first, and it needed completion in Shyler's Point.

When they reached the last stanza—"*...And the joy we share as we tarry there, none other has ever known*"— peace filled her heart. It wouldn't be easy to tell Pete she'd changed her mind. Wouldn't be easy to keep facing the town and their accusations. But God would give her the strength. He would uphold her and lead her from the shadows into the light.

People stood to leave, their shuffling feet loud against the wooden floor as they headed out the door. Tessy rose, too, and turned more slowly.

Pete leaned forward and took her arm. "I want to get an early start in the morning, so we need to turn in."

Tessy lifted her gaze to his and swallowed hard. "Pete, about goin' to Searcy—"

Pete turned to Jeremiah, who approached from the aisle. "Well, Preacher, you did well this evening. I believe my father would be pleased." Pete gave one of his haughty smiles—the kind that made Tessy cringe. "Of course, the delivery was a bit unconventional. But still effective."

Jeremiah leaned heavily on his crutch, as though weighted down, but his voice sounded strong. "Thank you. Effective is what I pray for." His gaze swung to Tessy, his expression tender, and immediately her heart increased its tempo. "Tessy, I wanted to wish you well in Searcy. I hope—" He swallowed, too, and tears brightened in his blue eyes before he blinked them away. "I trust that you will be happy there."

"I'm sure she will be, away from this town and their infernal ill-treatment." Pete's hand tightened on Tessy's arm. "We are planning to leave quite early, so if you'll excuse us."

Jeremiah stepped aside, but his gaze remained on Tessy's. "Good-bye."

Why did the tone hold longing? Tessy wished she could pull loose of Pete, stay and talk more, but Pete herded her along through the center aisle and out the doors. How she resented his high-handedness. The resentment rose in her belly, gaining intensity as she was forced to pound down the porch steps of the chapel. When they were halfway across the church yard, she finally found the courage to speak.

"Pete, stop a minute."

He kept going. "What is it?"

"It's about Searcy." She twisted her arm to remove his hand and dug in her heels. "I don't think I'm goin' after all."

"What?" The single word sounded as ominous as thunder.

She lifted her chin. "I need to stay here."

Pete crossed his arms. Evening shadows deepened his glower. "I thought this was all settled."

"It…it was." Tessy disliked the timidity in her tone.

She swallowed and spoke with more force. "But I made the decision for the wrong reasons. I was runnin' scared. But can't you see? If I got God on my side, there's no need for me to run. I need to stay here, face my shadows, and find my light."

Pete looked at her as if she'd lost her mind. "What are you babbling about?"

She'd long suspected that, despite Pete's upbringing in the church, he'd never developed a relationship with God. His response made her heart ache. "I'm talking about walkin' where God wants me to walk. There's a reason for me to stay here in Shyler's Point. I reckon there's reasons for me to go, too, but I need to do what God wants me to, not what you want me to." She linked her hands beneath her chin. "Please don't be angry."

Pete huffed. "I offer you the opportunity to make a change, to improve yourself, and you turn me down for some ridiculous notion about walking in the light? Perhaps it hasn't occurred to you that the sun shines in Searcy, too." Sarcasm laced his tone, stinging Tessy like a slap.

She dropped her gaze for a moment, praying for courage. "God wants me here. I have to stay."

"Fine." The word was fired like a rifle shot. "Stay here. It's nothing to me. I'm sure it will simplify things for me, not having to worry about you. Stay here and rot. Because that is what will happen. When Ma and Pop are gone, who will take care of you? The fine people of Shyler's Point? Bah!" His eyes hardened. "Don't come running to me then, Tessy, because I will not be your keeper."

Humiliation struck. He thought she needed a keeper? "I won't."

"Good. Then we understand each other." Abruptly he swung away and walked toward the cabin, his head held high.

Sadness slumped her shoulders. His rejection hurt. But she'd made the right choice. Even so, worry niggled. When Mama and Pop were gone, who would she have? She straightened her spine. She would have God. He was her Heavenly Father, her friend, her comfort and strength. He would be enough.

She lifted her gaze to the dusky sky and smiled. "Whatever You got planned, God, I'm ready for it. Help me get past these shadows. Help me find Your light."

"Tessy?"

She spun around, a hand on her chest. "Oh. Jeremiah." Her words came out on a sigh.

He approached slowly. "I didn't mean to intrude, but I couldn't help noticing that you and your brother were having some sort of difficulty." He paused. "Are you all right?"

Tessy sighed. "Pete and me…well, we never agree, so I'm used to it."

Jeremiah hitched closer and touched her arm. "I'm sorry. It's hard to be separated from family."

She blinked rapidly against tears. "Yes, it is. Even when Pete and me are in the same room, we're separated. That's why I should've known that goin' to Searcy with him wasn't a good idea. Can't change a lifetime of being miles apart."

Jeremiah frowned. "Can't? Or won't? I don't know what's created this distance between you, but I do know that nothing is impossible for those who believe."

Tessy gaped at him. "You tryin' to get me to move to Searcy?"

Jeremiah reared back. "Goodness, no. That's a decision you have to make for yourself. What I'm trying to say is that if you want a relationship with your brother, then some effort has to be made. It's a choice. You can let him go and say, 'Okay, then, I won't ever be close to him', or you can decide, 'Even if he's far away, I'll try to keep in touch.'"

Tessy tipped her head, curious. "You're far away from your family. You were even farther away when you were over in Europe. How did you stay in touch?"

Jeremiah lifted one shoulder in a shrug. "I wrote letters every week. Sometimes to my folks, other times to my brothers. But the contact was there."

Tessy's heart sank. She couldn't write. "It's impossible..." She hadn't even realized she'd spoken aloud until Jeremiah responded.

"It *is* possible, Tessy. Are you willing to make the effort?"

She raised her chin and set her jaw in determination. "Yes."

15

After Pete returned to Searcy, Tessy enjoyed two full weeks of peace. No one reported any items missing, so a cautious calm settled over the community. Although she still felt watchful eyes on her back, no one uttered unkind speculations. Pop was doing better, gaining strength day by day. Doc Winters thought he'd be on his feet and ready to stand in the pulpit in another two or three weeks. She rejoiced that her precious father was doing well.

Each day she and Jeremiah met beside the pond where the beavers had finished their dam and often sunned themselves in plain sight, their grunting chatter intruding and making Jeremiah laugh, for lessons in reading and writing. Those times were best, quiet times in study and conversation. She'd never met anyone as easy to talk to as Jeremiah. She considered him her best friend, and she treasured every moment spent in his company.

On this sunny mid-August Tuesday morning, her heart thumped happily as she moved across the heavy grass toward the pond. Her pack with her Bible, pad, and pencils bounced against her back. She could hardly wait to show Jeremiah what she'd copied last night.

"Isaiah 41:10, 'Fear not, for I am with thee: be not dismayed; for I am thy God: I will strengthen thee; yea, I will help thee; yea, I will uphold thee with the right hand of my righteousness.'" She spoke the words aloud, relishing the sound and feel of the syllables on her tongue, delighted that she could find them in her Bible, read them with her own eyes, copy them in her own hand. Pride filled her chest at the realization of how much she had learned in the short time Jeremiah had worked with her. He was a good teacher, but she was a good student.

She emerged from beneath the trees and entered the small clearing. Jeremiah was already seated on the familiar rock with his back to her, his plaid shirt taut across his shoulders, his dark hair glinting in the sun. Another feeling pushed at her chest—a feeling she knew she had no right to, yet it pressed on unheedingly.

Over the past weeks, Jeremiah had filled out, and he seemed to sit straighter than when he'd first arrived. The haunted look behind his deep blue eyes had dimmed. Tessy's heart beat in hopefulness that his inner shadows were fading.

He turned, and his welcoming smile warmed Tessy

clear through. "Well, hello! I thought you might not be coming today."

Tessy skipped the last few feet and seated herself in the grassy clover at the base of the rock. "Pop was up and about this morning, so I stayed and visited with him. Sorry I made you wait."

He shrugged, pulling in a deep breath and then releasing it. "Waiting here isn't a problem. It's a beautiful view, and I had companionship." With a grin, he pointed to one lone beaver perched atop the dam. The animal's brown beady eyes seemed to study Jeremiah. He gave Tessy a sweet smile. "I'm glad to hear your father was up. He must be doing better."

"Lots better." Without warning, sadness swooped through her. When Pop could preach again, Jeremiah would leave. She didn't want him to go. Shyler's Point would seem empty without him. She removed the pack from her back, wishing she could remove her sorrow as easily, and rustled through it for the writing she'd done the night before. She thrust the pad at Jeremiah. "I'm doing better, too. Look."

Jeremiah flipped open the pad and his eyebrows shot up. "Tessy! Your writing has improved so much. The letters are all neatly spaced, very readable. And you found these verses on your own?"

She nodded, pride washing through her. "Look what else I done—I mean, *did.*" She removed a folded paper from the pack and handed it over. As Jeremiah scanned it, she blurted, "It's a letter to Pete, tellin' him what all I've been learning. I know there's spelling mistakes. Would you fix 'em for me? I'll copy it over and send it right."

Jeremiah beamed at her over the top of the letter. "There are very few mistakes. I'll gladly make corrections for you, but I have to tell you how proud I am of you. You have made as much progress in a few weeks as most people make over several years. You're one of the smartest people I've ever met."

Tessy's jaw dropped. Smart? Her? Tears spurted in her eyes, spilled over, and slid down her cheeks.

His brows furrowed in concern. "What's the matter?" He touched her shoulder, and the letter dropped to his lap.

She covered her face with both hands while tears washed away the pain of feeling stupid and useless. She wanted to tell him they were happy tears, but her throat was blocked and all she could do was wait for the storm to run its course. When at last she uncovered her face, she found him watching, his dear eyes mirroring worry.

She gave him her brightest smile, tears cooling on her cheeks. "Nothing is wrong. I always thought I was too dumb to learn. But you said I'm smart. Like Pete. I'm smart."

"Of course you're smart." His confident tone humbled her. "Think of the knowledge you possess about the wildlife and forest plants. Only a smart person could hold all of that in her head. And your drawings are amazing. You're very smart, and I'm proud of you."

Fresh tears welled to the surface, but she smiled through them. "Thank you. I'm proud of me, too."

He leaned forward and placed a kiss on her forehead. The gesture seemed so natural that for a few seconds she didn't react, then the reality of what he had done struck. Heat climbed from her neck to her hairline. The spot of skin his lips had touched tingled as if lit from within, and she turned her gaze quickly aside to hide her flushed pleasure.

Jeremiah's cheeks glowed red. He straightened and swung his gaze to the beaver, which now snoozed contentedly. He cleared his throat, wiping beads of sweat from his forehead. "Mighty warm out here."

Tessy hid a smile. He wasn't fooling her any. Those blushing cheeks weren't from the sun's heat. The kiss meant something to him. Jeremiah liked her. Not just as a student or a member of the congregation. He liked her as a woman. Even if he had to leave, even if she never saw him again after he left Shyler's Point, she would carry the memory of his kiss forever in her heart.

He harrumphed again, loudly enough to rouse the sleeping beaver, and plucked up her letter with stiff movements. "Now. Let's take a look at this…" He assumed a tutorial air, his chin held high, his voice deep and serious.

But when their eyes met, a softness lingered there that belied his stiff bearing.

She found it very hard to stay focused on the formation of letters and correct spelling and where the period belonged at the end of a thought. When he'd corrected all the errors, Tessy tucked the letter away to copy over at home that evening. She retrieved her Bible and held it out. "Where should we read today, Jeremiah?"

He laughed.

She drew back. "What's funny?"

He swallowed his chortles. "I'm sorry, but it sounded as if you were asking if we were going to read something in the book of Jeremiah."

"We could." Tessy gave a slight shrug. "Haven't been in that one yet, but I did find it so I could learn how to spell it."

A grin crept up Jeremiah's cheek. "Oh?"

Her face flooded with heat. "Or maybe Joshua. Haven't done any reading there, either, but I remember Pop reading stories about the Israelites dividing up their land into the twelve tribes. Might be good reading."

Jeremiah nodded, his eyes still twinkling. "You're right. Turn to Joshua, and let's see how far you can go."

Tessy sat cross-legged in the grass, made a nest of her skirt, and rested her Bible in the folds. Turning the thin pages carefully, she found the first chapter of Joshua and began reading. She read slowly and steadily, pausing occasionally to glance at Jeremiah for confirmation on pronunciation of certain names and places, yet she thrilled to the fluency of speech she had gained already.

She came to verse nine. "'…Be strong and of good courage; be not afraid, neither be thou dismayed: for the Lord thy God is with thee whithersoever thou goest.'" She bit down on her lower lip. "Jeremiah, where will you go when Pop is able to preach again?"

He rubbed one hand up and down his thigh. "To be truthful, I'm not sure. I've come to love these mountains." His gaze swept over the peaks in the distance, traveled down the Old Muddy, and returned to her face. "Being here has been comforting. Yet I know my time is nearing its end, and I need to be making plans."

He leaned a palm on the rock and stared at the sky. "I got a letter yesterday from Reverend Dmitriev, the minister of the Russian Baptist church where I served before coming here." A shadow seemed to pass over Jeremiah's eyes, and Tessy found herself leaning toward him, her heart stirring with empathy even though she wasn't sure what troubled him. He paused for a long time, his face twisted into an expression of pain. Tessy held her breath, wondering what unpleasantness he was reliving.

Finally he sighed and rested his elbows on his knees. "When I was in Europe, I became involved in something illegal. Morally, it was right, but legally it was wrong."

"You couldn't have done anything so bad." She took

hold of his hand. "You don't have the heart for wrong."

Gratitude shone in his pain-filled eyes. "Thank you, but I'm not sure the leaders of Germany would agree with you. You see, I helped Jews."

What was so wrong with that? She'd never met a Jew, but they were God's chosen people. Jeremiah, as God's minister, would want to help God's chosen people. "So?"

He squeezed her hand. "I helped Jewish children escape. While the German army attempted to round them up and send them to work camps or to their deaths, I smuggled them onto Red Cross ships and sent them secretly to America where they now live with American Jewish families. I broke the law."

His face contorted. "And it was all so…so futile. So many people in need of help, so many people left behind, so people dead because I couldn't do enough." He slapped at his braces, and tears sprang into his eyes. "My weak legs couldn't hold up. They had to send me back because my weak legs couldn't hold up. And people died." He ended on a ragged whisper.

Tessy rose onto her knees and embraced him the way she would a child in need of comfort. She held him tight. Jeremiah's shadow was darker than hers. His was a shadow of guilt carried unfairly. So she held him, rubbed his back, pressed her cheek against his.

His arms came around her, too, clinging as though she held him together. Although she knew his soul was in torment, she was grateful for the opportunity to offer this bit of solace. She could repay him for the kindness he had shown to her.

In time he pulled away. He ran a finger beneath his nose and snuffled. Tessy sank back onto the grass close to his feet, but she placed a hand on his knee, maintaining contact. He put his hand over hers, linking fingers with her.

Tessy asked, "That letter you got, it didn't condemn you, did it?"

He shook his head. "The letter told me what's happening with the Jewish people since Germany has surrendered." His hand tightened. "They're are coming back to their homes, released from the prison camps, to find that others have taken over their homes or their homes have been destroyed." He released a humorless snort. "Ironic, isn't it? They survived war's atrocities only to be left without a place to live. Reverend Dmitriev told me about camps going up to house the Jews—DP camps, they're called, for displaced persons."

"Displaced persons…" Tessy's heart swelled in sympathy. So often she felt displaced, like a person without a place of belonging.

Jeremiah grimaced. "Think of it, Tessy. Young people locked away for the duration of war without being provided schooling. Now they're grown, but they have no way to care for themselves, no skills. What will happen to them? Reverend Dmitriev has been traveling to the various camps, offering his services as a minister." He sighed. "I would like to help. But how? The church won't send me back. I was sent home because of poor health. They won't risk me becoming ill a second time. And I don't have the funds to go myself."

"What would you do there?"

"Preach. Teach." He smiled. "Your success as a pupil has made me think perhaps I could teach others, as well, although my Russian and Polish is pretty limited. Still, it seems as if there should be something I could do for them." He heaved a mighty sigh. "How I'd like to be able to help those people. Perhaps make up for what I couldn't do the last time…"

He'd shared his heartbreak with her. She'd never been so honored. She wanted to find a way to help him see that he hadn't failed, or somehow make it possible for him to go back so he could appease his aching conscience. She didn't know yet what she would do, but she would pray. She would ask God to help her do something that would ease his pain.

"Jeremiah, I—"

"Preacher! Preacher, where are you?" A child called from the woods.

Jeremiah struggled to his feet, and Tessy handed him his crutch. Jeremiah fitted the crutch beneath his arm and hollered. "I'm by the Little Muddy!"

In a few moments, young Jimmy burst through the trees and ran, panting, to Jeremiah. The child's face was red, his freckles glowing, and he wore a smile from ear to ear. "Preacher, Doc sent me to tell ya. Heard on the radio that Japan surrendered! The U.S. dropped a big ol' bomb on 'em, and they gave up! The war's over!"

"What?" Tessy's heart nearly stopped beating.

The little boy threw his arms around Jeremiah's middle. "My brother'll be comin' home! Wait'll you meet him, Preacher!" Then Jimmy pulled back and twisted his face toward Tessy. "Oh, yeah. Your ma says come home right away. Your pa's took a turn."

"Pop?" Her elation at the previous news changed to dread. "What's wrong with Pop?"

"Don't know, but your ma says hurry."

16

Jeremiah waited with Mrs. McCleary and Tessy as Holden examined the older minister in the bedroom. The two women stood without speaking, almost without breathing, one pressed on either side of him. They both seemed to gain strength from his presence, so he remained quiet, inwardly praying, as they waited.

The moment Holden appeared in the opening of the main room, Mrs. McCleary left Jeremiah's side and rushed to the doctor. "I don't understand it, Doc. He was up walking around the cabin this morning. Went all the way to the outhouse and back without any help. Then, after lunch, he said he didn't feel right. What happened?"

Tessy pressed closer, and Jeremiah took her hand. Her fingers were cold.

"It's a secondary infection." Though Holden's voice was calm, lines of concern furrowed his brow. "This happens occasionally to surgery patients, especially when they do too much too soon. I imagine Paul was up a bit more than was wise while Pete visited. You must understand that your husband's body suffered quite a trauma when his appendix ruptured. It will take longer for it to mend."

Tessy was quivering. Her colorless face clearly spoke of fear. Jeremiah gave her hand a reassuring squeeze, but she didn't respond.

"But he'll be okay?"

Before Holden answered, Tessy pulled away from Jeremiah and ran out the door. Jeremiah went after her. He stepped outside the cabin and followed the sound of sobbing. He found her hunched over the washtub, crying as though her heart would break.

His chest clutched in sympathy. Hitching up behind her, he placed his hand on her heaving back. "Tessy, your father is a strong man and Holden is a good doctor. Your father will be all right."

Tessy shook her head, her honey hair swinging wildly with the movement. "It's because of me."

Jeremiah frowned. "What?"

She shot to her feet and moved to the other side of the washtub. Her white face was pinched with torment. "I did it to him."

If the man was worn out from Pete's visit, how could it be Tessy's fault? "You didn't have anything to do with this setback."

She nodded, her chin quivering. "I did! This morning I thought how you'd be leaving soon as Pop was well, and I thought how I didn't want you to go yet." Her voice rose in pitch. "I made it happen by wishing you wouldn't have to go!"

Could she truly believe she was capable of inflicting illness on someone with a simple thought? Up until now he'd believed Tessy saw herself as a jinx because others blamed her for sad events. But no one was pointing a finger of blame now, and still she assumed responsibility. All this time he'd seen the townspeople as the ones with superstitions. Now it appeared that Tessy was not only affected by their beliefs, she harbored them herself.

"Tessy, listen to me. Your thoughts had nothing to do with your father becoming ill again." Slowly he moved around the washtub, closing the distance between them. She stood with her arms wrapped around her middle, rocking herself and softly crooning. He thought his own heart might break, so palpable was her self-recrimination.

A jumbled thunder of voices intruded, and Jeremiah looked over his shoulder. A group of townspeople—little Jimmy, followed by the Spencers and Colt Murphy as well as several others—approached. In the middle of the throng Jeremiah spotted Callie, carrying baby Evangelina. Jimmy waved a small flag, and all chattered in obvious joy, their faces beaming.

The group moved to the side yard of the dogtrot, and Colt called out, "Hey, Preacher, we're all headin' to the Post Office for a celebration. Want to come along?"

The invitation didn't extend to Tessy. He shook his head as Tessy turned her back and dropped her chin, seeming to attempt to hide in plain sight. "You go on and enjoy yourselves. I'll come a bit later."

"Suit yourself." The group moved on, the cheerful chatter drifting away with the crowd's departure.

Jeremiah turned back to Tessy. "Tessy, please listen—"

But she was gone. During the brief seconds his attention was elsewhere, she had slipped away. He circled the yard, seeking. "Tessy! Tessy, where are you?" But she made no reply, and finally he realized she didn't want to be found. He released a sigh. Slowly he returned to the cabin to offer a prayer for comfort and strength for Mrs. McCleary and a petition for good health for the reverend. He also prayed for Tessy's safety and peace of mind.

Tessy ran through the woods, unmindful of direction or destination. Tears distorted her vision, turning her heedless race into a dangerous activity, but she didn't care. She had to take her ill wind as far away from home as possible. Maybe if she was far from her father, he would improve.

Her mind replayed the morning as her feet thudded against the ground. She had hummed on the way to meet Jeremiah. Pop took ill after she left the house. Had her happy tune summoned the evil spirits? *"Sing before seven, mourn by eleven,"* her granny had always said.

But it had been past seven, she reminded herself. The sun had risen well above the horizon. The time should have been safe, so maybe it wasn't the humming. It had to be her longing for Jeremiah to stay in Shyler's Point. Her errant thoughts jinxed her father and made his illness recur. The guilt was nearly unbearable.

A sharp pain in her side brought her up short. She gasped and clutched her ribs. Breathing heavily, she forced herself to walk a slow circle until her breathing returned to normal and the pain subsided. The physical pain slipped away, but the sorrow in her heart remained. *Oh, Pop, I'm so sorry...*

Looking around, she realized she was close to Ol' Gordy's valley. It had been weeks since she'd seen the old man, yet she hesitated about visiting him. If she went down, would she carry bad luck to him? Loneliness stabbed. Fresh tears stung her eyes. She didn't want to be alone.

The Lord thy God is with thee whithersoever thou goest.

She frowned, carefully considering the message. Tipping her chin upward, she squinted at the sky. "Are You here, Lord? I don't like being alone. Are You with me?"

"I'm here, Missy." Ol' Gordy waited several feet in front of her, partially hidden by a low-hanging forsythia branch.

Despite her tears, she smiled, his stooped shoulders and prickly chin a welcome sight. "Hey, Ol' Gordy."

"Hey, Missy. What you doin' out here talkin' to the sky?"

Tessy shook her head, stepping forward slightly. "Wasn't talkin' to the sky. I was talkin' to God." She slipped into hill talk, a match for Ol' Gordy's simple speech.

He snorted. "Not much point in that, I reckon. He's all a-tangled up somewhere's else. Leastwise, allus seems to be somewhere's else when I need somethin'."

His melancholy tone pricked Tessy's heart. "What do you need? Can I help?"

The old man smiled, but his faded eyes looked sad. "Ah, you're a good girl, Tessy McCleary. You got a heart big as my mama's. Allus wantin' to do good an' brighten up somebody's day. Yep, you're a good girl, Tessy."

Her face fell. "If you only knew…"

Ol' Gordy stepped close and touched her arm with a wizened hand. "If'n I only knew what?"

She ducked her head and brought up her shoulders, like a turtle sinking into its shell. "It's my pop. He's took sick again. An' it's my fault."

His expression turned hard. "Who tol' you that?"

"Nobody told me. I just know."

198

"Ain't true." His prickly chin thrust forward belligerently. "You ain't equipped for evil, Missy. Couldn't be your fault. Gotta be somethin' else."

"But what?" Tessy wanted Ol' Gordy to be right, but it was so hard to believe. "He was fine this mornin', up walkin' around and laughin', askin' for hot cakes and syrup. Then all of a sudden he's sick an' ailin' again." She lowered her gaze. "I did it by thinkin' too hard about the new minister, Jeremiah."

Ol' Gordy released a huff of laughter.

Her head shot up. "It ain't funny, Ol' Gordy. My pop's bad off."

The old man shook his head and squeezed Tessy's arm. "I'm not laughin' about your pop, Missy. I'm laughin' at what you said. You're a fetchin' young lady, an' you're thinkin' on a man who's caught your eye. No harm can come from that." He paused, his wrinkled eyes fixed on Tessy's. "You got deep feelin's for this man?"

Tessy bit down on her lower lip. But Ol' Gordy must have read the truth in her eyes, because he smiled gently and gave her arm another squeeze.

"Nothin' bad comes from deep feelin's, Missy. You didn't bring nothin' bad on your pop."

"How can you be sure?"

"Just am." He removed his hand from Tessy's arm and shook his head, his eyes turning dreamy. "Like my mama. Tender heart, feelin' responsible. Ain't right... Just ain't right… They gotta pay."

Tessy frowned. "Ol' Gordy?"

He gave a start, and his expression cleared. He swiped a hand across his chin. "Been awhile since we've set an' chatted. You come on down to my cabin an' I'll fix us some mint tea. You can tell me more 'bout this new minister."

Tessy followed Ol' Gordy down the rough pathway to his cabin. The steep mountain sides blocked even the high, early afternoon sun, and Tessy shivered despite the warmth of the day.

Ol' Gordy turned with a broad smile when they reached the bottom and swung his hand toward the cabin door. "Set yourself down. Won't take long to get water boilin'."

Tessy sat at the rough table and rested her elbows on its edge. Plunking her chin in her hands, she watched Ol' Gordy stoke the fireplace and swivel an iron arm holding a kettle over the blaze. He turned, caught her watching, and gave a smile.

"It's gonna be okay. Your pop'll be fine, an' them people in that town—they'll figger out you ain't no ill wind. You wouldn't be feelin' none of this hurtin' inside if'n them people hadn't put that brand on you." He blew out a harsh breath. "Bah! Any ill wind belongs to them an' their high-falutin' ways. None of 'em worth a hair on your head, 'ceptin' maybe them two ol' ladies what live in the house behind your'n."

Tessy straightened. "Do you know Miss Vivian and Miss Viola?" Although Miss Vivian had become a missus in her later life, Tessy had spent all of her growing up years referring to her as "miss," so it felt natural.

He harrumphed. "Nah. Not really." He lowered his bent frame onto the stool across from Tessy. "Met 'em a coupla times when I was young. Nice ladies. They had a nice brother, too. He helped my ma once, fixed her plow so's she could cut the ground for plantin'. Didn't charge nothin', neither. Nice man."

Ol' Gordy referred to Callie's father. He'd been gone a long time. She tipped her head. "Ol' Gordy, how long 've you lived in this valley?"

"M' whole life. Was born right here in this cabin." His gaze swept the tiny room, pride shining in his eyes. "Ain't much, but it's all mine. My pa claimed it, an' my ma worked to keep it. Reckon I'll die here, too."

"Please don't talk of dyin'." The thought made Tessy sad. With Jeremiah certainly leaving, Ol' Gordy was her only friend.

The old man chuckled. "Ah, now, Missy, I got too much to do to be thinkin' of dyin' yet. Figger I'm too ornery to die. Angels'll hafta to wrestle me off this earth. 'Sides, got me some scores to settle. They'll pay..." The faraway look returned, making the hair on the back of Tessy's neck prickle.

"What do you mean?"

Ol' Gordy stood. "I'll git that tea now. Mint leaves make a good flavor with the comfrey."

She'd get no more out of him. It was best to let the subject go. But curiosity pressed at her. Who did Ol' Gordy mean by "they"?

17

Jeremiah stayed at the McCleary cabin. Outside, the town celebrated the official end to the war with Japan. Laughter and the banging of pots and pans continued throughout the day while inside the cabin a different type of war waged. He prayed with Mrs. McCleary, assisted Holden in sponging the feverish patient, and offered emotional support to Reverend McCleary's wife and doctor. And all the while, he kept an ear tuned to Tessy's return. His worry mounted as evening approached, dark fell, and still Tessy had not come back. Where could she be?

Although the reverend's fever ran high through the afternoon, shortly after supper his temperature began creeping back downward. While Holden didn't completely drop his guard, he did admit he was pleased to see this change. Finally, when the sliver of moon hung high and white in the blackened sky, Holden heaved a sigh.

"I believe he'll rest through the night. You get some sleep, too, Anna. I'll be back early in the morning to check on him. If anything changes, clang the bell. I'll come running."

Holden had already told Jeremiah about the emergency bell hanging on the back corner of the post office. The post office was just a short distance from the cabin, so neither Mrs. McCleary nor Tessa would have to venture far in the dark to ring the warning if needed. But Tessy was already out in the dark now. Her mother needed her. What was keeping her away?

Mrs. McCleary hugged Holden. "Thank you. Don't know that I'll do any sleeping until he's well again."

Holden patted her shoulder. "Now, Anna, it won't do for you to become ill, too. Lie down and sleep. The draft I gave Paul will keep him comfortable for several hours. So you sleep. Doctor's orders."

The woman nodded, her eyes sad. "I'll try. But with Paul, and now Tessy..." Her brow furrowed. "We all know Tessy isn't fond of the dark. She must be very upset to stay out at night."

Jeremiah shot Holden a concerned look. He wanted to ask if Holden thought something had happened to Tessy, but he didn't want to worry Mrs. McCleary further.

"You know Tessy sees the woods as her own back-yard." Holden spoke soothingly, his tone light. "She's probably sitting under a tree, enjoying the sounds of nature and praying for her father. She'll come home when she's ready."

Mrs. McCleary sighed. "I suppose you're right…"

"Jeremiah and I will pray she comes home quickly." Holden grinned. "And when she gets here, give her a good talking to about running off during family emergencies."

Mrs. McCleary chuckled. "Oh, yes, Doc, I'll tell her how I feel about it."

Jeremiah intended to share a few thoughts on Tessy's disappearance, as well, the next time he saw her. She shouldn't worry people this way. He and Holden bid Mrs. McCleary good-bye and stepped out into the early evening. The temperature had cooled, but the air felt sticky. Cabin lights glowed, and from behind closed doors the sounds of celebration continued.

"People are certainly happy to see the war end," Holden said.

Jeremiah nodded. "Jimmy was sure excited. He said his brother would be coming home."

"Several families in the community will see their boys return. The celebration will rise again, I'm sure, with each soldier's arrival."

Wind swept down the mountain, carrying a swirl of leaves. Jeremiah watched the ground, placing his crutch carefully. "Did Shyler's Point lose many young men in the war?"

Holden shook his head. "Seven of the eight who marched off will march home again. I'm happy Callie had a little girl. I can't imagine watching a son head off into battle." He swiveled his gaze in Jeremiah's direction. "Were you close to the fighting? It must have been a terrible thing."

Pictures flashed in his mind. He grimaced. "You were on Oahu when the Japanese bombed Pearl Harbor. You know how awful it is."

Holden's forehead crinkled. "But what you witnessed must have been even worse. Civilians under attack—unarmed women and children. That isn't an equally-matched battle. That's a massacre."

Jeremiah's chest went tight. He wished he could erase the memories from his mind. He longed to do something now to help the survivors. But what could he do with his crippled legs and limited funds?

The men passed the church, and a resounding pop, like rifle fire in the distance, intruded. Jeremiah's blood ran cold and he froze, his heart pounding in alarm. "What was that?"

Holden stopped, too, his gaze angled toward a leafless oak that towered over the church. The empty branches swayed in the night breeze. Another loud *pop-pop* sounded. Holden pointed. "It's the dead oak tree. I've got to get some of the men to cut that thing down. One of these days a strong wind is going to send it tumbling, and I don't want anyone to get hurt." He gave Jeremiah's shoulder a light clap. "But not tonight."

Jeremiah heaved a sigh. Only a dead tree branch—not gunfire. The war was over. If only he could put it to rest in his memory. The men continued to the Winters' house and entered the gate. Halfway across the yard, a moan echoed from the peaks beyond Shyler's Point. The hair on the back of Jeremiah's neck stood up. It was only the wind, but it sounded like crying. Like mournful wails of lost souls.

Jeremiah shivered. He was beginning to dislike the dark, too, just as Tessy did. Was she somewhere on the mountain, hurt and crying? Or had she holed up in a safe place, intentionally hiding away? Another soulful moan drifted from the mountain.

Holden held the door open. The welcoming glow of a lamp invited Jeremiah to hurry and enter the house.

Jeremiah struggled up the steps and dropped onto the swing. "I think I'll sit out here and pray for the McCleary family again before I turn in."

Holden paused, his hand on the door. "Try not to worry about Tessy, Jeremiah. She's as familiar with the woods as I am with this little house and yard. She'll be back in the morning, apologetic for worrying her mother."

Jeremiah smiled. "I know."

Holden disappeared inside the house. The screen

door clicked as Jeremiah closed his eyes. For long minutes he sat, listening to the night sounds on the mountain. He enjoyed the crickets' song as well as the gentle hoot of owls, but the sad moan of the wind made his heart heavy. He began to pray, sometimes petitioning, sometimes praising, sometimes questioning. He ended with, "Father, wherever Tessy is right now, keep her safe from harm and bring her home again. Amen."

Tessy awakened with a start, the crackle of a fire intruding in her restless dreams. She lifted her head from the hard surface of a table, surprised to discover she was in Ol' Gordy's cabin.

Her heart beat in panic—what time was it? The cabin was gloved in gray, the only light from the small fireplace where coals glowed and the remains of a log weakly burned. The log popped, sending up a small flurry of sparks, and she jumped. She crossed to the planked door, opened it, and peered outside. Nightfall, a high sickle moon, full dark. How could she have been so foolish as to fall asleep? Mama would be beside herself with worry.

She closed the door and scanned the small cabin. Ol' Gordy's rope bed scrunched in the corner, a worn quilt covering the lumpy mattress, but the old man wasn't in it. He wasn't anywhere.

Opening the door a crack, she peeked out into the dark. Her heart pounded fearfully at the complete blackness surrounding the cabin. No shadows—there wasn't enough light to cast a shadow. The wind howled, trees rustled, and a lone coyote called from the distance. Gathering her courage, she called, "Ol' Gordy, you out there?" Her voice sounded higher than normal, choked with fear, and she knew it wouldn't carry above the sounds of the wind. If Ol' Gordy was out there, he was probably asleep. Closing the door again, she wrapped her arms across her middle and crossed to the small fireplace.

A jumble of cut wood lay heaped on the floor next to the stone fireplace. She picked up two small logs and thrust them into the flame. She hunkered in the front of the fire, watching the dancing yellow and orange tongues lick across the wood.

The room was warm, but still she shivered. How could Ol' Gordy live in this dreary little cabin by himself? Although she had never been surrounded by companions, loneliness struck harder here than it ever had before. She needed to visit Ol' Gordy more often. Surely he felt secluded out here.

Her thoughts wandered over the mountain and to her cabin. Was Pop better? Had Doc been able to help him? What must Mama be thinking with Tessy still gone? Guilt assailed her. She shouldn't have stayed away so long. And Jeremiah would be so disappointed in her for running off. Yet at the moment, it had seemed the only thing to do—to get far away and take her ill wind with her. Jeremiah didn't believe she carried an ill wind. Neither did Ol' Gordy. But then why did bad things happen?

Something banged outside the cabin. She leaped up and pressed her back against the rough wall, holding her breath. The door slowly opened, creaking on rusty hinges, and a bent-over figure toting a sack crept slowly inside. Tessy recognized the gray head, and she released her breath in a whoosh. "Ol' Gordy, where have you been?"

The old man straightened, his faded eyes wide beneath his tangled gray hair. The bag dropped to the floor, and he slammed the door with a hard thrust of his hand. "Missy, you awake?"

"Yes." Tessy stepped away from the wall. She glanced the bulky burlap bag. "What've you been doing?"

Ol' Gordy scratched his chin with gnarled knuckles. "Huntin' mushrooms."

"But it's blacker'n coal out there. An' you don't even have a lamp. How could you find them?"

A strange smile crossed his face. "I have my ways…"

When Ol' Gordy didn't wish to answer a question, it remained unanswered. She sank down on a stool. "Sure scared me to wake up here all alone. Can't believe you let me sleep. My ma's probably sick with worry. You shoulda sent me home."

Ol' Gordy shuffled across the room, lifted a blanket,

and tossed the bag into the recesses of a small cave. A damp, musty odor wafted through the room, making Tessy's nose twitch. The bag thumped as it landed, followed by a *tink*, and she wondered what the bag hit.

The old man dropped the blanket back into place then seated himself at the table. His hair stood on end, and he had a strange glimmer in his eyes. But his smile was calm. "I figgered you needed a good rest. Didn't mean for nobody to worry over ya. With your traipsin', figgered people'd trust you to know what you're doin'."

Tessy lowered her chin as another wave of guilt washed over her. How could people trust her when she had proved herself to be so untrustworthy? Mama and Pop had needed her, and instead of staying to help she had run away. Ol' Gordy had welcomed her company, and she'd fallen asleep. Jeremiah had befriended her, and she'd sneaked away when he wasn't looking. She didn't deserve anyone's trust.

"Missy, I can take ya back to town now, if'n you want."

She couldn't go out into that jet black night. "No. Not 'til the sun rises."

The old man gave a nod followed by a coarse cough. Heaving a deep sigh, he pushed himself to his feet. "Wal, I reckon that's not too far off. You jest stretch out on my bed there, an' I'll snug up on the rug at the fireplace. We'll head you out at daybreak."

"I'll stay here at the table. You take your bed." Tessy

couldn't imagine the arthritic old man lying on the floor and getting any sleep at all.

But Ol' Gordy waved a bony hand. "I've slept in worse places." He sank down in front of the fireplace and curled himself to fit on the worn braided rag rug. He pressed his fist against his mouth and coughed again—a deep, hacking sound. The cool night air must have been hard on him. At last he quieted and seemed to drift off.

Tessy crossed to the bed. A corner of yet another burlap bag stuck out from beneath the flap of quilt draped on the mattress. She pushed the bag out of sight with her foot and lay down. The ropes squeaked as she turned onto her side and curled her hands beneath her head. *Let Mama and Pop sleep sound, Lord.* She closed her eyes and slept.

When Tessy awakened, the fireplace held only a pile of cold ashes. Ol' Gordy still lay curled on the floor. She rose stiffly, stretching to entice her muscles into motion. She tiptoed to the window and peered out. Although shadows still shrouded the valley, the sky appeared pink over the mountains.

Ol' Gordy snored softly, his spindly body pulled into a question mark. She removed the quilt from the bed and placed it over his inert form. He snuffled, coughed again, but didn't rouse.

She should leave him a note. Pride swelled at the realization that she was capable of writing a note. But she hadn't brought her pack, and she didn't see anything in the cabin on which to write. Besides, he would know where she'd gone. She opened the door, cringing at the creak of the hinges, and stepped out into the cool morning. Less than two hours later, she stepped through the dew-laden grass of her own backyard.

When she entered the house, Mama looked up from her place at the kitchen table. Relief flooded her face. She rose and held out her arms. "Oh, Tessy, darlin', thank goodness you're all right."

Tessy raced into her embrace and clung. "I'm okay, Mama. I'm sorry I stayed out all night. I planned on coming back, but I fell asleep, an'—"

Mama pulled away to take Tessy's cheeks in her hands. "Hush, darlin'. I have to tell you something. It's something bad."

19

J eremiah had just finished asking a blessing for the meal when someone pounded on the front door. At once Evangelina began to wail.

"I'll get the door," Holden said.

"I'll get the baby," Callie said at the same time.

Jeremiah struggled to his feet and followed Holden. From the sound of the knock, someone had an emergency. He hoped it didn't involve Reverend McCleary.

Holden opened the door, and Colt Murphy barged in. He swept his hat from his head and held it against his chest with both hands. "'Mornin', Doc."

"Good morning, Colt. What brings you over so early?"

The town's acting sheriff heaved a deep sigh. "Well, Doc, I was just checking to see what's been stole from your place."

"Stole?" Holden glanced over his shoulder at Jeremiah. Jeremiah offered a helpless shrug while his heart began to pound in trepidation. Holden turned back to Colt. "I'm not sure what you mean."

Colt bounced his hat against his thigh. "I've been runnin' all over town this morning, collecting reports on a number of thefts that took place sometime during the night."

Callie entered the room cradling Evangelina. "All over town?"

Colt snorted. "Some way to celebrate the war's end, huh?" He reached into his shirt pocket, withdrew a small notebook, and squinted at the page. "Fourteen different houses hit. An' I don't figure I'm done. Figure there's plenty who haven't discovered they're missin' something yet. That's why I'm going door to door. So…" He slipped the pad back in his pocket. "What about you folks? Anything?"

Callie handed the baby to Holden and entered the kitchen. Jeremiah's heart thudded as he waited for Callie to make the rounds. In a way, he hoped Callie would find something missing. Tessy wouldn't steal from the Winters—she had too much respect for the doctor and his wife—so if something was missing from this house, it would indicate Tessy's innocence.

Callie returned. "Honestly, Colt, I can't find anything amiss."

Colt nodded. "If you find out later that you've overlooked something, give me a holler, would you?"

"I certainly will."

Colt paused for a moment, a speculative gleam in his eyes. "Funny thing about this thieving. Yours, Callie's aunts', and the reverend's place are about the only ones that ain't been hit at some time. Sure makes a person wonder..." He plopped his hat into place and departed.

Holden turned a scowl on Jeremiah. "You don't think Tessy went around last night and—"

"No, I don't." Jeremiah spoke more forcefully than he had intended.

Holden grimaced. "I'm not accusing her, but she did take off, and she was very upset. Could it be possible?"

"Absolutely not. And I think it would be better if we didn't mention how Tessy took off yesterday to parts unknown." Jeremiah clenched his fists. "These self-righteous finger-pointers don't need more fuel for their unwarranted fire."

Callie sighed. "Jeremiah, neither of us want to believe that it's Tessy doing the stealing, but even you have to admit it seems suspicious."

Jeremiah shook his head. "I've spent a lot of time with Tessy recently. Part of the reason is so I could follow her, see if she was the one stealing things from around town. I've never seen any indication she is capable of that kind of deviltry."

Holden and Callie exchanged a glance.

The hair on Jeremiah's neck prickled. "What?"

Callie patted the baby's back. "Jeremiah, since you started spending time with Tessy, no one has reported a theft. There are some who think it further proves Tessy's guilt. How can she steal when she's with the preacher?"

Jeremiah gawked. "So my effort to prove her innocent has actually helped to prove her guilty?"

"Not by everyone's accounts. We just thought you needed to know what some are saying." Holden gave the baby to Callie and put his hand on Jeremiah's shoulder. "You and Tessy have become friends. Are you sure your fondness for her isn't clouding your judgment? Is it possible Tessy could have taken things to get even with townspeople?"

Jeremiah stumped away, his heart pounding in his throat. Was it possible? The thieving had stopped when he had begun spending part of each day with Tessy. He had no idea where she'd been all night. Could he know for sure she didn't creep around the town, taking items that didn't belong to her?

He squeezed his temples, forcing the thought away. She was gentle and kind. Revenge wasn't in her. But the fact that he questioned her innocence for even a moment made him realize how difficult it would be to convince the town.

He shook his head. "She didn't do it. I'd bet my crutch and braces on it."

Holden's expression turned grim. "I hope it doesn't come to that."

Tessy buried her face in her hands, torn between relief that Pop rested well during the night and fear over the sheriff's visit before she'd returned. She hadn't done any stealing, but who would believe her? Especially after Mama confessed Tessy had spent the night away from home.

Mama led Tessy to the kitchen table and they sank into side by side chairs. She squeezed Tessy's hands. "Did anyone see you who could tell Colt where you were all night?"

Ol' Gordy didn't want people nosing around. Tessy couldn't say anything about him. The sheriff would go pester him, and she'd lose her friend. Miserably, she shook her head. The lie pricked deep. How she hated dishonesty. But what else could she do?

Mama sighed. "Well, then we'll just have to hope for the best. Hope Colt turns up something that points a finger elsewhere. In the meantime, you get cleaned up. You're going to stick close to home 'til this thief is caught. We can't have people blaming you for anything else."

Panic struck. "I can't stay cooped up in the cabin."

"I need your help here with your father. You can write another letter to your brother. Plenty to stay busy with here 'til this all blows over. It's for the best."

Someone knocked on the door, and fear ignited in Tessy's chest. Mama opened it, and the fear dissolved at the sight of Jeremiah Hatcher, the familiar crutch tucked under his left arm.

"May I come in?"

Tessy shot to her feet as Mama stepped aside. "Certainly, Preacher." He entered, and she stood beside the open door, wringing her hands. "I wasn't expecting you this morning. Figured Doc Winters would stop by, but…" She drifted off, her gaze flittering back and forth between Tessy and Jeremiah.

"The doctor will be coming shortly." Jeremiah aimed his gentle smile at Tessy. "I'm glad to see you're home. I prayed you would be here, safe and sound."

"I'm just fine." Tessy licked her lips. She'd made such a ninny of herself, running off, but she didn't want to apologize with Mama there as an audience.

Jeremiah took a step forward. "I was worried. I—" He glanced at Mama, who remained by the door listening and watching. "Could we step outside for a moment and speak privately?"

Mama moved to the breezeway. "Yes, you two talk. But stay in the cabin, Tessy. I'll go check on your father."

Tessy scuttled to the window and pulled open the shutters. She sucked in a big breath of the fresh air. How would she bear being stuck in the cabin until the thief was caught? It had been busy for months. She wished she could dash into the woods again.

Jeremiah clumped up behind her. "I need to talk to you about what happened yesterday."

She gripped the windowsill. "What about it?"

"Before you took off, you said something that bothered me."

She picked at a splintering bit of wood "Oh? What did I say?"

A sigh wheezed past her ear. "Will you at least look at me?"

Tessy hung her head. She was being unreasonable. Slowly she faced him. The sun streaming through the window brought out hints of burnished copper in his dark hair. His blue eyes appeared even deeper in hue, the dimple in his left cheek pronounced. He was so handsome. Why did he bother with her? A man like him could befriend anyone. Why spend time with an illiterate jinx?

He smiled. "Thank you."

Her heart fluttered. "You're welcome." She hugged herself, keeping her hands trapped lest she reach out to him.

Jeremiah's expression turned serious. "Tessy, yesterday before you ran off, you said that you were responsible for your father's illness. You don't believe that, do you?"

Her arms still tight across her middle, she shrugged. "Maybe."

"Why?"

"Plenty of folks around here have seen it. They believe it."

"First Corinthians 3:19 says that the world's wisdom is foolishness in God's eyes." Jeremiah thrust out his chin. "This jinx business is foolishness."

"Seems to me you've been a little foolish about something, too." Tessy cringed, surprised by her boldness.

His eyebrows shot upward. "Oh? What have I been foolish about?"

"You been blaming yourself for what others did to the Jews. But from the way I look at it, you helped more'n most. Ain't—isn't there a verse somewhere in Second Corinthians that says something about God appreciating what a man does rather than being angry about what he doesn't do, long as he's doing his best?"

Jeremiah's Adam's apple bounce up and down. She'd rendered him speechless. She found a certain pleasure in having made a good point.

He sucked in his lips, making the dimple deepen. His eyes sparkled, and she got the impression he was holding back a chuckle. "You're absolutely right, Tessy. God does look on the heart and sees the motives of men. He knows when we strive for evil or good." He leaned forward a bit, locking gazes with her. "Tell me the truth. Did you intend for something bad to happen to your father?"

Tears stung. She shook her head.

"Did you intend for anything bad to happen to anyone else in town?"

"N-no."

"Then you aren't responsible." He held out his hand. She clasped it. His warm palm pressed firm against hers sent a delightful feeling through her. "Your heart is a heart meant for good, not evil."

It was her turn to be struck speechless. That this man—this good, Godly, revered man—should say such a thing to her... Without conscious thought, her body leaned toward him. He responded with one faltering step forward. But before they could embrace, another voice intruded.

"Glad to see you're here."

19

Tessy yanked her hand from Jeremiah's grasp and clutched it to her bodice, her wide-eyed gaze pinned on someone behind him.

Jeremiah turned and found Colt Murphy in the open doorway. "Hello again, Mr. Murphy."

"Preacher." Colt nodded in Tessy's direction. "Need to talk to Miss McCleary."

Jeremiah took two awkward steps that put him beside Tessy. Fear emanated from her tense body, and his chest tightened with sympathy. He wouldn't abandon her. "I suppose this is about last night's upheaval?"

"Yep." Colt's eyes narrowed, his gaze turning hard. "An' whether she's the one who created it."

"I didn't take anything." Tessy's fingers convulsed on the fabric of her dress.

Colt sauntered to the center of the floor. "S'pose you tell me where you were last night. Your ma told me you weren't in your room."

Jeremiah placed his hand on Tessy's quivering back. "Tell the truth, Tessy. Nothing bad can come from telling the truth."

Tessy shot him a panicked look, then faced the sheriff. "I was on the mountain."

"All night?" Colt's voice was harsh, pressing.

She nodded.

"Those the clothes you wore?"

She glanced down at herself. "Yes, sir."

Colt looked her up and down. "Seems to me that if you slept on the mountain, there'd be evidence of it. Dirt smudges, maybe remnants of dried leaves or grass in your hair. The dress is wrinkled, but that don't speak of sleeping on the mountainside—just speaks clothes bein' worn too long maybe. Hair needs a brushing, but that would be normal for morning." His gaze dropped to her scuffed oxfords which were covered with mud and bits of grass. "Guess your feet show evidence of lots of traipsing, though."

Tessy's face turned white. Jeremiah pressed his fingers against her shoulder blade. Where had she been last night? What had she been doing? She remained silent, her chin quivering, but she kept her gaze locked with the sheriff.

Colt crossed his arms. "I can see you aren't gonna be helpful. 'Less you tell me exactly where you were, I'm gonna have to—"

"Now wait a minute." Jeremiah stepped forward. "Did any of the people who reported missing items see who took things from them?"

The sheriff glowered. "'Course not. Thief came sneakin' around in the middle of the night. Nobody up watchin' at that hour."

Jeremiah spoke softly, not wanting to make an enemy out of this burly man. "I'm not trying to tell you how to do your job, but it seems that you're jumping to conclusions. Just because Tessy wasn't in her room last night doesn't mean she was creeping around town taking things. She says she was on the mountain all night." He squared his shoulders. "And I believe her."

Colt released a huff. "Preacher, you're new around here. This girl—"

"She hasn't been given a chance to defend herself. To-day, or in the past." Jeremiah gestured to Tessy. "I've tak-en the time to get to know her, and—"

"Oh, yeah." The sheriff's lips twisted into a knowing leer. "I heard how you been keeping an eye on her, keep-ing her busy so she wouldn't have time to do her thievin'."

Tessy's eyes flew wide and her mouth fell open.

Jeremiah bristled. "Now wait just a minute. I—"

"An' it worked…for a while." Colt crossed his arms, his gaze hard. "But you weren't watchin' her last night, and she had a hey-day, didn't she?" His disparaging gaze roved from Tessy's head to toes. "Look at her. Disheveled, feet covered with muck, dark circles under her eyes. She wasn't sleeping on any mountainside, but instead was up all night, roamin' around, snatching whatever she could get her hands on."

Jeremiah gritted his teeth. "You've already found Tessy guilty without an ounce of real evidence. Have you seen her take anything? Have you found any of the missing items in her possession? No. You're assuming, Colt. Instead, you should be looking for the real thief."

The man shook his head. "You just can't see it, can you, Preacher? Well, you'll figure it out in time, just like the rest of us have." He pointed a beefy finger in Tessy's direction. "You stay put, girl. No more wanderin' off. I want you where I can keep an eye on you. Understood?"

Tessy gave a brief nod and lowered her chin.

The sheriff clomped out of the cabin.

Jeremiah touched Tessy's shoulder. "Tessy, I—"

She leaped away as if his touch stung. "What Colt said... Did you take time with me to watch me? To see if I was stealin'?"

The betrayal in her eyes broke his heart. How could he explain his motives in a way that wouldn't crush her?

Tears pooled in her eyes, making them appear huge and luminous. "I thought you wanted to be my friend. I thought you wanted to help me, an' all the time—"

"I want to be your friend." He held out his hand in entreaty. "I want to help you. I started spending time with you to prove to everyone that you weren't the one stealing, but then—"

"So you were keeping an eye on me, like Colt said…"

Jeremiah growled. "It isn't the way he made it sound. How can I make you understand?"

"I do understand." She swiped her hand across her eyes, removing the shimmer of tears. "I knew when you came it wouldn't last. I knew the town would get to you. I knew, so it's okay."

"No, it's not okay!" Anger laced his tone, anger at the community that planted seeds of self-recrimination in this tender-hearted young woman and at himself for watering them. "It's not what you're thinking. Please listen to me."

She moved toward the breezeway, her gray eyes wary. "I can't listen to no more, Jer—Preacher." Her tone was flat, lifeless. "Mama needs my help with Pop." Turning on a heel, she ran.

For a moment he considered going after her, but common sense overrode emotion. She wasn't ready to listen to reason. He needed to give her time to calm and to get some rest. Reluctantly, he left the cabin and headed for the church. He'd go where it was quiet, and he'd pray.

His steps dragged, his heels heavy. *Heavenly Father, I've failed again…*

Tessy slammed the door to her room then threw herself across her bed and gave vent to the hurt pressing like a boulder in her chest. She'd trusted him. He said he was her friend, and all the time he was only watching her, waiting for her to slip up so he could let the others know.

Tears rolled down her cheeks as she replayed every conversation, every moment with Jeremiah. The sweetness of their time together was now bile on her tongue. How could she look at him again and not feel like a fool?

Rolling from the bed, she dashed away her tears. She stomped to her dresser and yanked open the top drawer. She'd remained in Shyler's Point because Jeremiah was going to teach her. She'd learned more that she wanted to. No reason to stay anymore.

She took out her writing pad and pencil and flopped them on the dresser top. She chose a fresh sheet and began to write.

Dear Pete, if you think you can find me a job in Searcy I am reddy to come there. I know you probly cant come til the week end and thats okay. I will have things packed and reddy. Hole bunch of stuff got took last night and Colt thinks I took it but I dint. I need to go away from here before anything else turns up missing. I will be waiting. Your sister, Tessy.

She folded the page to fit an envelope. As she put her writing pad away, her gaze lit on the drawing pad, open to the picture of the beaver's dam. She picked it up, her mind replaying Jeremiah's look of pleased surprise when she'd shown him the drawing. With a trembling finger, she traced the words he had written at the bottom of the page. He'd said she was talented, called her gift. She closed her eyes, reliving the warmth that had washed over her with those words. But he hadn't meant it. He was only cozying up to her, getting her to trust him.

The warmth turned cold. She grasped the corner of the page, prepared to rip the paper from its pad and tear it to bits. But she paused. Very carefully she pulled the page loose. She rubbed out Jeremiah's neat print from the bottom of the page and rewrote it with her own block letters. Then, impulsively, she folded the drawing and put it in the envelope with her letter to Pete.

She glued the envelope closed and addressed it. As she laid it on her dresser top, she caught sight of herself in the mirror. What a mess. She washed her face, combed her hair, and changed her dress. Then she peeked in the mirror again. Although she couldn't erase the evidence of tears from her bloodshot eyes, her overall appearance was much improved. She snatched up the letter. She'd ask Mama to walk her to the post office.

Jeremiah closed the doors to the chapel, struggling with a gust of wind that worked against him. Once the latches were secure, he grasped the railing and descended the steps. His gaze on his black shoes, he didn't realize he had company until he reached the bottom and raised his face to find Callie waiting a few feet away with a blanket-wrapped bundle in her arms.

The wind tousled her hair, and she pushed the errant locks behind her ear. "I guess you felt the need for some prayer time, hm?"

In spite of himself, Jeremiah laughed. "Word gets around fast in a small town."

Callie shrugged, grinning impishly. "Most times everyone else knows your business before you do."

He stepped near and peeked into the bundle. Evangelina's blue eyes peered back. Jeremiah touched the soft tuft of hair that fell to a point on her forehead. "She's sure getting her feathers…"

Callie gave him an odd look. "What?"

He chuckled. "Never mind." He sighed. "Sure am glad she wasn't born on a Friday the thirteenth…"

Callie's face clouded. "Jeremiah, about Tessy—"

He held up a hand, "I don't want to discuss Tessy right now."

"Are you sure? Sometimes it helps to share your burden with a friend."

Her concerned expression and inviting tone tugged at Jeremiah. It would feel good to share this burden. He was so weighted down. What was God's will for Tessy? He wished he knew.

Callie touched his arm. "Two heads are better than one. Let's sit down and chat, all right?"

They moved to the steps. Callie sat and placed Evangelina in her lap so the baby's feet pressed against her tummy and her little head rested on Callie's knees. Jeremiah lowered himself to the next higher step, his legs stretched straight in front of him. He leaned on his elbows. Wind swept down from the mountain, carrying wild scents and chasing the dust along the roadway. Jeremiah wished it would sweep away his gloomy thoughts.

Callie fixed Jeremiah with an attentive gaze. "What happened with Tessy?"

"I think she gave me the boot." Jeremiah huffed. "Colt said he knew I was 'watching' her, and I could feel the change in the air. She doesn't think she can trust me now." He scowled. "And I can't blame her. I must seem like everyone else in town—like I think she's a jinx, too."

Callie sat quietly.

"Tessy has changed so much in the past few weeks. She's reminded me of a flower slowly opening up to the sun. Do you know she actually quoted scripture to me this morning?" He nodded at Callie's raised eyebrows.

"She reminded me of a passage in Second Corinthians about God looking on a man's intentions and finding them pleasing when the heart is right, even if the works fail."

"I can't imagine Tessy being brave enough to spout scriptures to a minister. But what an appropriate passage."

Jeremiah hung his head. "Then Colt made his comment, and I watched her fold in her petals and shield herself again." His throat went tight. "She ran off and refused to let me explain."

Callie sighed. "Colt probably took her by surprise. Once she's over the shock, she'll think about the Bible words she spoke to you and remember that your heart was right. Tessy will forgive you and be willing to be your friend again."

He shook his head. "You didn't see her. She looked so betrayed."

Callie started to speak, but a strange squeal that seemed to come from the sky interrupted. She looked up, and Jeremiah twisted on his seat, too, scanning the area, his heart rising into his throat.

The huge oak beside the church swayed in the strong breeze. The squeal changed to series of *pop-pop-pop*, and a resounding *crack!* exploded. The large limb extending over the church roof broke loose from the trunk. Pushed by the relentless wind, it seemed to hover above them, falling in slow motion.

"Callie, look out!" Jeremiah threw himself over Callie and the baby. Callie shrieked, the baby wailed, and the crash of the branch couldn't bury their cries of fear.

20

Oh, Lord, please let Callie and the baby be all right…
Had he spoken the words or only thought them? Jeremiah wasn't sure, but they were fervent. His legs were twisted to the side, his arms coiled around Callie. She lay motionless on the steps beneath him. The wailing wind tossed smaller branches of the limb back and forth. Each motion forced sharp twigs into Jeremiah's back, but despite the pain he didn't think he was seriously hurt.

"Callie? Are you all right?" He squeezed her arm, shaking it a bit.

She shifted her head slightly. "I…I think so. I'm just stuck."

"What about Evangelina?"

The baby emitted a high-pitched cry of obvious fury.

Callie released a half-laugh, half-sob. "I think she'll be okay."

Jeremiah sighed. "Thank God."

Pounding feet and frantic voices reached them. Someone yelled, "Go get Doc! Who's under there? That you, Preacher?"

Jeremiah recognized Mr. Spencer's deep voice. "Yes. And Callie Winters and her baby."

"You hurt?"

"I don't think so. We just can't move, and the baby's trapped underneath Callie."

"Someone get some rope and pulleys." Mr. Spencer took charge. "We gotta lift this branch off of them. Did someone go after Doc?"

Another breathless voice answered, "He's comin'. Hang in there, Preacher and Callie—we'll get you loose."

It seemed hours passed as Jeremiah waited beneath the limb, trying to hold himself up to prevent pressing his weight on Callie or the baby. His back stung where the branches cut through his shirt, and his muscles ached. But he held on, alternately praying and talking softly to Callie. Evangelina continued to cry in a weak, hiccuping wail that was music to Jeremiah's ears.

At last the heavy branch lifted, and a cheer erupted. Jeremiah rolled away from Callie to collapse, muscles quivering, against the chapel steps. Holden scooped up Evangelina and assisted Callie to her feet.

Callie pressed her face against Holden's neck, holding tight. The beauty of their embrace brought a fierce longing to Jeremiah's chest. Then she pulled back. "I'm all right. Nothing more than bruises. Check on Jeremiah. He shielded Evangelina and me, so he took the force of the limb."

Holden placed a kiss on her forehead, kissed the baby, and laid the infant in her mother's arm. He knelt beside Jeremiah. "Well, Preacher, let's check you out." But before Holden could begin an examination, a ruckus broke.

"There's the cause o' this! You brung this on, Tessy McCleary!"

Tessy and Mrs. McCleary stood on the periphery of the gathering. Tessy clasped her hands to her chest. Her gray eyes were wide, and Mrs. McCleary's face was pinched and white.

Jeremiah struggled to sit upright. "You can't blame Tessy for this. Holden told me the tree had been struck by lightning months ago. The branch was dead. It was only a matter of time before it fell."

The speaker advanced on Tessy and others trailed him, all with dour expressions. "You stay out of this, Preacher. You ain't been around long enough to know this girl's ways. She was born on a Friday the thirteenth an' trouble's been followin' her all her life long."

Tessy's chest rose and fell in panicked breaths. Jeremiah thought his heart might break as he witnessed her fright.

"I—I didn't mean anything."

"You never mean nothin," another man broke in, "but

it don't change it. People got hurt. An' the church roof is gone!"

Jeremiah's heart sank. A section of the roof was gone. The limb must have bounced off the corner of the roof before landing on him and Callie. He shivered, realizing how seriously they could have been hurt had it fallen directly on them. He pointed. "Look. If—"

"Tessy McCleary, this wouldn't've happened if you hadn't been out dallyin' with the preacher!"

Blood pounded in Jeremiah's ears. "That's enough!"

"Don't deny it, Preacher." The man whirled on him, his face contorted with rage. "I seen you two comin' in from the woods, both smilin' and lookin' pleased. That's dallyin', in my book."

"There's been no dallying!" Jeremiah wished he could spring to his feet and take the man head-on. "You want to blame something, blame the wind!"

A stout breeze whisked down the mountain, tossing people's hair, teasing skirt and jacket hems, and carrying bits of leaves and the scent of fall in its wake.

Another man pushed through the crowd. "We know it were a wind—an ill wind brought on by that Tessy. Look at the roof! Don't need no other proof 'n that."

Tessy cried out, "I'm sorry! I didn't mean it!" Her tear-filled gaze lit on Jeremiah. The sorrow in her eyes pierced him. "I'm so sorry…" Then she ran up the road toward her house, her mother following.

Holden turned to the crowd, his expression grim. "You men, start cutting up that limb. Maybe the physical exertion will bring down your tempers. Our concern right now should be making sure the preacher and my family are unhurt and getting the roof fixed before weather damages the inside of the church. Standing around spouting accusations about who's to blame accomplishes nothing."

The men milled aimlessly, softly grumbling amongst themselves. Holden shouted, "What are you waiting for? You've got saws and a sturdy limb—use that wood for new shingles!"

The man who had accused Tessy and Jeremiah of dallying swung to face Holden with a fierce glare. "I'll make sure the roof gets fixed, Doc. But you make sure that man don't try to stand behind the pulpit again." He stabbed an accusing finger in Jeremiah's direction. "Anybody cavorts with Tessy McCleary's ilk ain't fit to be speakin' God's word."

Jeremiah lay on the exam table while Holden tended the gouges on his back. He didn't know what stung more—the antiseptic or the remembrance of the words spewed by the man in the church yard. Not fit to speak God's word? How many others in the community shared the view but hadn't voiced it? How could he walk the streets of Shyler's Point without wondering who was whispering behind his back?

"All done." Holden clamped his hand on Jeremiah's shoulder. "Try not to dwell on what Ted Maness said. The man is a known hot-head, and everyone's emotions were flying pretty high with the excitement. Things will calm down."

"The way they have for Tessy?"

"That's different."

Jeremiah sat up and faced Holden. "How is it different? The town branded her a jinx. The town's now branded me unfit to preach. Both accusations are unfounded an' unfair." His southern twang came through as his voice quivered with righteous indignation.

Holden grimaced. "The men were distraught. Don't assume that everyone in town seconds Ted's opinion."

"No one spoke up in my defense." Jeremiah clenched his fists. "Just as no one has ever spoken up for Tessy." Callie entered the room. Worry furrowed her brow, but he was too angry to soften his tone. "It's high time someone stood up and let these people know that what they're doing is *wrong*. Since no one who lives here has the courage, an outsider will have to do it."

Callie bit her lip. "Jeremiah, we talked about this."

He took a deep breath, an attempt to bring his temper under control. "I know, but I can't stay silent." He lowered his chin, memories storming his mind. "When I was in Europe, I sneaked around, helping Jews in secret. So many were left behind, so many died because I was limited by secrecy."

He met Callie and Holden's solemn gazes. "I can't help wondering, what if I hadn't done my work in the shadows? What if I had been bold enough to march through town in the light of day, openly denouncing the treatment of the Jewish people? Would others have stood with me? Would others have helped? Could more have been saved?" He held his hands outward. "I'll never know, because I didn't have the courage to do it."

Dropping his hands to his lap, he pulled in a breath. "I'm not going to sneak around in shadows anymore. I'll stand up and declare what is happening here is wrong and must stop. It's too late to help the Jews in Europe, but it isn't too late to help Tessy. She's as undeserving of the town's treatment as the Jewish people were undeserving of Hitler's rampage. It can't go on."

Callie and Holden stood silently for long seconds. Then Callie nodded. "I'll stand beside you. I should have done it long ago. I kept hoping…" Tears filled her eyes. "By staying silent, I've been just as guilty as those who have spoken against Tessy."

Holden clasped Jeremiah's shoulder. "I'll stand with you, too."

Gratitude swelled in Jeremiah's chest. If the town reacted adversely, it wouldn't affect him. He'd leave soon.

But Callie and Holden would remain here, facing possible censure. They were braver than he.

"Thank you." He slid from the table and positioned his crutch. "Now if you'll excuse me, I have a sermon to prepare."

Tessy gazed at the open drawing pad on her dresser. Had her letter and picture reached Pete? How long 'til he came to get her? A week? Maybe two? Could she last that long holed up in this cabin? She wouldn't leave it. Colt said not to, but mostly she couldn't risk running into Jeremiah. Hurt too much…

She sank onto her bed and lifted her Bible from its place on the side table. She lay in it her lap, letting it flop open. Her eyes fell on an underlined verse in Psalms 119.

"'Thy word is a lamp unto my feet and a light unto my path…'" As always, her heart lifted in pleasure at her newfound ability. She backed up several verses and read, "'Oh, how I love the law! It is my meditation all the day…'" She closed her eyes. "Oh, thank You, God, that I can read the words myself. I *do* love this law…"

A picture of Jeremiah seated on the rock beside Little Muddy, an open Bible cradled against his thighs, appeared behind her closed lids. She willed the image away, but it remained—his gentle face lifted in a smile, his blue eyes shining with pleasure, his dark hair glinting under the sun. How readily he had accepted her, reached out to her, taught her. Then he had betrayed her.

The pain stabbed. "Why, God?" Tessy slumped over the Bible. "Why'd he do it? I trusted him. I thought he was my friend. I thought he wanted to help me. But all the time..." She dashed away her tears with an impatient swish. "I want to believe what he said, that he saw me as a gift, not a dimwitted jinx, like everybody else. But it's so hard."

She opened her eyes and located the verse in Psalms again. She read on, her finger guiding the way. When she reached verse 101, her heart clutched. "God, I've tried to keep my feet from evil ways. How come others can't see it?" The unfairness slammed into her, bringing a new rush of tears. "Why do they blame me for things I didn't do?"

Her thoughts drifted to her conversation with Jeremiah about his secret work in Poland and Russia. The German leaders blamed the Jews for things they hadn't done, either, and had treated them unfairly. "Some men just don't have a heart for right..."

Why were some so determined to do evil while others did good? People in town paraded through her mind—people who had rejected her, called her names, shoved her aside... A few had offered kindness—Ol' Gordy, Viola and Vivian, Doc and Callie. And the preacher man.

She resisted adding Jeremiah to the list, the heartache of his duplicity still fresh. Yet she couldn't ignore him. He had opened her heart to friendship and her mind to learning. "And he hurt me so much, too…"

Sighing, she sought comfort in the Bible. "'I have not departed from thy judgments: for thou hast taught me.'" She stopped, her head snapping up in realization. "Thou hast taught me… *Thou* hast taught me…" Understanding washing over her.

Tessy shifted the Bible to the mattress, dropped to her knees beside the bed, and folded her hands over the open Book. "Forgive me, God. All this time I've been wantin' to credit Jeremiah with teaching me. But You brought him here, You let him reach out to me, You opened my head and my heart to learning what letters strung together mean. You helped me trust him. Must've been You—I never trusted nobody before, except Ol' Gordy."

She pressed her forehead against her clasped hands. "I don't understand why he betrayed my trust, but I thank You for sendin' him here, for opening me up to reading so I can keep finding more light in the pages of Your Word. No matter what other people do, I'll keep learning, God—I'll keep learning even when I'm in Searcy—an' I'll always follow Your path. Show me Your light, God, so I'll know how to follow."

Jeremiah appeared in her memory once more. Tessy swallowed hard, pushing past the sadness that threatened to overwhelm her. "And, God, shine a light for Jeremiah, too, to help him find his way back to Europe. His heart is there, with the people in those camps. You gave him his tender heart, God. Isn't right that he should feel so helpless and unworthy. Let him go back, God. You can make the way."

Peace flooded through her. "And, God, help me find new friends. Don't let me close myself away. Now that I know what it is to have a friend, I want to have it again. Guide me to friendship with people I can trust, please. Amen."

As she rose, Ol' Gordy drifted through her thoughts. He was a friend who had never betrayed her. She was his only friend, and she would leave soon. Guilt assailed her. She couldn't leave without saying good-bye to him. Ol' Gordy had encouraged her to get off of this mountain, to go where people would treat her kindly. He'd be proud of her for finally finding the courage to go. First thing in the morning, she'd head to his cabin and spend the day with him, have a picnic by the bubbling creek, say her good-byes.

Her gaze fell again on her drawing pad. She'd give him the picture of the purple saxifrage since he liked it so much. A proper good-bye to Ol' Gordy, then no more leaving this cabin until Pete came for her.

21

The swing chains creaked a raspy morning song. Jeremiah cradled a coffee mug between his palms and inhaled deeply of the mixture of coffee, pine needles, decaying leaves, and wildflowers—a heady perfume.

Homey sounds, Callie's and Holden's soft voices and the baby's coos, drifted from the other side of the screen door. Jeremiah imagined Evangelina in Callie's arms, her dimpled hands reaching toward her mother's beaming face, Holden leaning over the back of the chair to touch the baby's head. A happy, heart-lifting scene. Callie called him "Uncle Jeremiah," making him a part of the family circle, but the truth was he didn't belong here.

Displaced persons… The description from Reverend Dmitriev's letter haunted him. He needed to write back to the Russian minister, to offer words of encouragement and perhaps a promise to help. But he'd tried to help the Jews during the war and failed. He'd tried to help Tessy and failed. How could he be of any help to anyone? Jeremiah had never felt as crippled as he did at that moment.

"Dear Lord in Heaven, let me be used by You…"

He set the mug aside, took up his crutch, and made his way down the porch steps to the backyard where the view of the mountains was unhindered. He drank in majestic layers of green and bold splashes of gold, ginger, and russet from the changing leaves on oaks, maples, and sumacs.

When he'd arrived in Shyler's Point, he'd hoped the glorious view of God's handiwork would bring healing to his bruised heart. In ways it had. His soul had been touched. He felt God's presence here. But new bruises rested on top of those healing underneath. Was it possible to find complete healing?

A mockingbird called, its sweet melody easing the ache in Jeremiah's heart. He lifted his head, seeking the singer, and his gaze swept across the sky. His lips twitched as a smile teased, a verse coming to mind. *The heavens declare the glory of God; and the firmament sheweth his handiwork.*

He sent a wink skyward. "Well, God, the firmament is particularly charmin' this morning, all turquoise where it meets the mountains, robin's egg blue straight overhead, and' a bright yellow sun shinin' strong and proud. I admire your paint palette."

Standing in the splash of sunlight, surrounded by

beauty, peace curled through him. Things weren't perfect, but God was there. He would need the Lord tomorrow when he stepped behind the pulpit and spoke the forecful words he'd scribbled in a writing pad. Folks wouldn't like his message. But he'd give it anyway. They had it coming.

A movement to his right caught his attention, and he squinted against the bright morning sun. A glimpse of a blue gingham dress and shining honey hair slipped into the stand of maples. Tessy. He frowned. Was she escaping again? The need to talk to her, to make things right, rose within him. If they had some time alone away from the town and its finger-pointing, maybe she would be willing to listen.

Clumping to the edge of the porch, he called through the screen, "Holden? Callie? I'm going for a walk. Don't expect me any time soon."

"Do you want to take some food with you?"

A picnic lunch might be nice, but it would take time to pack, and Tessy was already well ahead of him. "Thank you, Callie, but I'll be fine. I'll see you later." He headed for the break in the trees where Tessy had disappeared.

Pride filled Jeremiah as he stood on the mountain pathway, his eyes sweeping over the distance covered in the past two hours. His traipsing with Tessy had increased his strength and endurance. He'd kept Tessy within his sight and remained on her trail. She'd entered a ramshackle cabin nestled at the shadowy base of the mountain in a narrow valley. The steep downward climb now awaiting him seemed daunting, but he'd come this far. He would make it the rest of the way.

Leading with his crutch, he allowed his feet to slide. He caught hold of tree trunks to help steady himself as he made slow yet unremitting progress toward the cabin. At last he reached the bottom of the incline. As he crossed the patch of thick grass to the cabin, Tessy's sorrowful voice reached his ears.

"You should've come to me. I would've helped you."

A mumbling male voice—gruff and croaky with age and weakness—answered, but Jeremiah couldn't make out the words.

"'Course you deserve help! How can you say somethin' like that?"

Tessy's obvious distress compelled Jeremiah to hurry. His crutch slipped, and he fell flat on the cabin's rickety porch.

Moments later Tessy bent over him, her eyes wide with disbelief. "What're you doing out here?" She looked toward the trail, then at him again. "You followed me?"

Jeremiah nodded, his breath coming too hard to reply.

"Scared I was going off on another thievin' spree?"

She crossed her arms and glared, her gray eyes snapping.

Jeremiah pulled himself upright by gripping the rough hewn porch post. "I wanted to make sure you were all right. I know you aren't a thief."

She picked up his crutch and handed it to him. "Did you hurt yourself?"

Jeremiah shook his head. "Who's inside the cabin?"

Tessy's chin quivered. "My friend, Ol' Gordy. And he's really sick. I…I think he's dying."

She rushed into the cabin, and Jeremiah followed. She knelt next to an old rope bed, where a man lay on filthy blankets. His sunken cheeks, gray pallor, and glassy eyes spoke of a serious illness. He wheezed with every breath. Pneumonia? Jeremiah feared the man wasn't long for the world.

He stepped near the foul-smelling bed and took the man's hand. "Gordy? I'm a friend of Tessy's."

Gordy's red-rimmed eyes focused blearily on Jeremiah. His lips were cracked, the lower one caked with dried blood. "Friend o' Missy's? So you'll take care o' her for me? You'll finish my revenge?"

"Revenge?"

The man tried to laugh, but it turned into a horrible cough. He flopped backward on the soiled blankets and gave a weak nod. "On them folks in town. I ain't gonna be able to finish. Still houses to go."

Tessy leaned close. "Ol' Gordy, what do you mean?

What've you been doing?"

Gordy licked his lips. "I been gettin' even with all them folks. They let my ma work herself to death—didn't raise a finger to help her. Didn't care nothin' for an ol' Cherokee squaw. So she wasted away…" He coughed again, a wracking cough that went on and on.

Jeremiah helped the man into a seated position. "Tessy, get him some water."

Tessy retrieved a dipper of water, but Gordy waved it away. "Won't do me no good." He fell across the mattress again. "Missy, want you to have Ma's embroid'ry squares from the trunk. Don't have nobody else to give 'em to. You take 'em."

Tears hovered on Tessy's lower lashes. "You keep them. They're yours."

The old man shook his head, his gray hair flopping. "Ain't got no use for'em now." He kept his gaze on Tessy who remained beside the bed, tears streaming down her pale cheeks. "I tried to make 'em pay, Missy. I took things 'cause they took from you an' my ma. They took her life. Tried to take your spirit. So I made 'em pay. Those things are hid 'round the cabin. Those're for you, too."

Jeremiah's pulse raced. This old man was the thief. He could hardly wait to tell Colt Murphy and all the other finger-pointers about Tessy's innocence.

"Goin' to meet my Maker soon. Won't get to stay in Heaven, but I hope He'll let me see my ma just once afore

He sends me on to the devil's keepin.'"

Jeremiah's heart constricted. How awful to know death was near and to be certain of eternal punishment. He sat on the edge of the bed. "Gordy, would you like to know how to spend eternity in Heaven with your ma and Jesus?"

He sighed. "Know how. My ma taught me. But I strayed too far. Done too many wrong things. Did'em a-purpose. God'll hafta punish me now."

Jeremiah gripped Gordy's dry, hot hand. "Did your mother tell you about the thief on the cross? Jesus told him, 'Today shalt thou be with me in paradise.' Confess your sin and ask for forgiveness. Ask Jesus to be your Savior, and you will be welcomed into Heaven."

Gordy's breathing was becoming more shallow, his hand limp. "Pray with me. Don't wanna die in darkness. The shadder o' death is comin' for me. I'm scared..."

Jeremiah closed his eyes and prayed aloud. "Dear Lord, I am a sinner..." Gordy's whispered, raspy voice echoed his words. Tessy's soft, reedy voice joined in. Then Gordy gasped.

Jeremiah opened his eyes. Gordy stared at the open doorway of the cabin. A smile lit his face. "Light... Chasin' away the shadder o' death..." He stretched out his hand.

Jeremiah looked toward the door. Shadows cloaked the entry, the sun hidden by the mountains. Gordy's hand dropped. His eyelids slid closed, and a final breath wheezed from his lungs. He was gone.

Tessy's face crumpled. "He was my friend, Jeremiah."

Jeremiah rose and took her into his arms. She sobbed softly against his neck, her arms wrapped tight around his shoulders. "He's in a better place now, Tessy. He's at peace."

"I know, but I'm gonna miss him something fierce."

They grieved together—Tessy for the loss of her friend, and Jeremiah for her heartache—for several minutes. Finally she pulled away, and he offered his handkerchief. She wiped her eyes, blew her nose, then set her shoulders in a determined manner.

"Ol' Gordy's parents are buried alongside the cabin, by the runnin' stream. I've put flowers on the graves many a time. Ol' Gordy would want to be with them. Can we dig him a grave and put him to rest?"

Jeremiah hesitated. "Shouldn't we have a decent funeral for him in town?"

She shook her head, her honey hair flying. "He had no use for the town. Only people he liked was Callie's aunts and pa. But Callie's pa is dead, and it's too far down here for Miss Vivian and Miss Viola to come. They probably wouldn't even remember him, anyway. Been years since he made his presence known around town. At least"— her face twisted in pain—"so's anybody would know he was there."

Although Gordy had intended to help Tessy, he'd caused her much grief. "Do you have any idea where he hid the things he took? Returning those items will absolve you of blame."

Tessy shrugged. "He tossed a bag in the little cave in the back of the cabin. It'd be a likely hiding spot." She looked down at the still body. "But I don't want to think about all that. I want to put him close to his ma and pa. He can sleep eternally there."

Jeremiah still harbored concern about simply burying a man without reporting his death, but Tessy was right about the old man's feelings toward the town. He'd prefer a simple burial without involving anyone else from Shyler's Point. "I'll look for a shovel."

"Cave's opening is right there." Tessy pointed to a blanket hanging on the back wall. "I'm gonna get some water and clean him up—find some other clothes. While you dig—" She broke off, swinging her troubled gaze in his direction. "Can you dig a grave, Jeremiah?"

He shrugged. "I've never done it before. But I'll do my best."

"I'll help."

His heart lifted. No complaint, no criticism. Only acceptance and a willingness to help. No wonder he loved her. The desire to take her into his arms and profess his feelings nearly overwhelmed him, but now wasn't the time, not while her heart ached. "I know you will help.

I'll start digging, and after he's cleaned up, I'll help you dress him for burial."

She threw herself into his arms and gave him a brief, heartfelt hug. When she pulled back, tears glittered in her gray eyes. "I'm glad you followed me. I need you right now."

He nodded, swallowing the lump in his throat. He needed her, too. He prayed he'd have the chance to tell her so in the near future.

22

Tessy's heart fluttered high in her chest even while it ached with sadness during Jeremiah's sweet prayer over Ol' Gordy's grave. So many emotions rolled through her, she could hardly hold them all. Sorrow for Ol' Gordy's death and his lonely life here in the dark valley away from everyone, relief that the stolen items could be returned, gratefulness for Jeremiah's presence. And love.

Love had blossomed in her heart for Jeremiah. But she couldn't tell him. He'd be moving on, all the way to Europe if God answered her prayers to pave the way, and she'd be going to Searcy with Pete. She'd always believed that when love for a man found its way to her heart, she would feel light and airy inside. Instead, her heart was weighted. She'd never have the happy ending the storybooks proclaimed. Their lives were too different.

"Amen."

Tessy met Jeremiah's gaze across the fresh grave. A

new rush of tears built, and these weren't for Ol' Gordy. She pushed the sorrow aside. "We should gather up the stuff Ol' Gordy stole so we can tote it to town."

He looked skyward. Deepening shadows had shrouded the valley in velvet gray. "It's hard to tell the time with the mountains blocking the sun."

"It's late afternoon already. We better hurry."

He swung his crutch around and moved toward the cabin. "I found some bags in the cave and more in the shed. I'll see what's in those. You search the cabin, okay?"

Tessy returned to the gloomy interior of the cabin. She crossed to the mantle and lifted down the lantern. To her dismay, it slipped through her trembling hands and shattered on the hard dirt floor. Now she would have to search in the dark. Fear held her captive.

"Lord, please help me." The words from Isaiah 41:10 whisked through her mind. The fearful trembling lessened and her pulse slowed. "Thank You, Lord."

Though the dark shadows still surrounded her, Tessy pushed through the gloom and located three bags hidden in various spots around the cabin. She tugged them to the porch. A rickety child's wagon lay upside-down in the grass, but it was too small to hold everything. The old man had been busy. It would take several trips to bring everything back out of the valley. She and Jeremiah wouldn't be able to do it alone.

"I'm sorry, Ol' Gordy, but I'm gonna have to bring

others down here. I hope you'll forgive me." He couldn't hear her words, but it made her feel better to talk to him.

A wind coursed through the valley, carrying the scent of rain. Urgency filled her. They needed to hurry. She closed the shutters on Ol' Gordy's window to protect his meager belongings and the things that had been stolen. Then she hurried around the cabin to find Jeremiah.

Tessy trotted across the ground toward Jeremiah. A bolt of lightning lit her tense expression. Thunder rumbled in the distance, and a few raindrops spattered his face. She stopped in front of him, wringing her hands.

"There's a storm brewing. Now isn't a good time for us to be heading for town. Lightning could catch us."

He grimaced. "We can't stay here all night. It wouldn't be…seemly." The two of them spending the night alone in the valley was out of the question. Besides that, he had a sermon to deliver in the morning.

Lightning lit the northern horizon and a louder roll of thunder followed. Her breath came in short spurts. "These storms blow up mighty quick, and they can be fierce. It's not good to be out in them 'cause that lightning is dangerous."

"Then we better get moving so we can beat the storm back to town." He pointed. "The storm's to the north.

We're heading south. It'll stay behind us if we hurry."

"I'm scared..." Her voice trembled like the leaves rattling in the breeze that seemed to gain strength by the minute.

Jeremiah squeezed her hand. "I know. But we won't walk through this storm alone. God's right here, too."

"It's getting so dark. And I broke the lantern."

Climbing the mountain in the gray shadows with his unsteady legs didn't leave him teeming with confidence, either, but his mama had taught him strength came from the Lord. With God's help, and Tessy's guidance, he could make it. If only she would find the courage to lead him out.

"Tessy, listen to me." Jeremiah tugged at her hand. "Tell me what you've discovered in the Word. What has God told you about fear?"

"Isaiah 41:10, 'Fear not, for I am with thee: be not dismayed; for I am thy God: I will strengthen thee; yea, I will help thee; yea, I will uphold thee with the right hand of my righteousness.'" Tessy's hand shook within the fold of Jeremiah's fingers, but she recited the verse with confidence.

He nodded, smiling. "God will strengthen you. Lean on Him. He'll guide you safely through the dark and into the light."

She looked toward the north where the black sky told of heavy rain. Lightning flashed, illuminating the entire valley for a brief few seconds. She gasped. "Jeremiah, if lightning keeps flashin' like a firefly, it'll help me see the pathway out. It'll be like a big lantern showing the way."

"Good thinking! Let's use that lightning for our good."

Tessy released Jeremiah's hand. "Okay, Preacher, we're gonna march up that hill. I'd appreciate you prayin' while we go, 'cause it's not gonna be easy."

"'I can do all things...'"

Tessy finished, "'...through Christ which strengtheneth me.'" She raised her pert little chin. "Come on, Jeremiah."

The wind pushed against their backs, peppering them with cold raindrops and the occasional ping of pea-sized hail, but they stayed ahead of the storm's fury. So much electricity tingled through the night it made her hair snap, yet the bright bursts of lightning were welcome.

Tessy tempered her steps with the sounds of Jeremiah's thrashing behind her. She paused occasionally, waiting on an illuminating flash of lightning to help her choose the smoothest pathway. Jeremiah's heavy panting filled her ears, the sound discernible over the roar of wind and rain behind them. *Dear Lord in Heaven, give him the strength to keep coming. Light my path so I can bring him safely home...* The prayer hovered on her heart as she stayed a few feet ahead of him—near enough to be seen, far ahead enough to not accidentally trip him with her heels.

The angry black sky hid any stars, but occasionally the clouds cleared enough for Tessy to glimpse the moon. The slice of white orb reminded her Who made the moon and the stars. If He was powerful enough to hang that big old moon-ball in space, then He had the power to get her and Jeremiah safely home again.

She glanced over her shoulder as rolling thunder reverberated through her chest. He hung on his crutch, his head sagging in exhaustion. Her heart turned over. "Jeremiah, you doing okay?"

"I'm okay. How far"—he paused, his chest heaving—"do you figure we have left to go?"

By her calculations they were more than halfway to Shyler's Point and Saturday was fading into Sunday. "A little over a mile, but we're done with the uphill. We'll be going mostly down now. Will that help?"

He chuckled. "Sure. Lay me on my side and give me a push. I'll just roll back."

Tessy grinned. He hadn't lost his sense of humor, so he wasn't defeated. A blast of wind swept down. Jeremiah took a stumbling step forward, and Tessy caught hold of his arm. Together they weathered the mighty downdraft.

Tessy released Jeremiah and he laughed. "What's funny?"

"There's a verse in Isaiah—the forty-first chapter, I think—that talks about God fanning the enemies of the people and the wind carrying them away. I thought for a moment that might happen."

Tessy gave the expected returning chortle, but then she frowned as another strong draft carried fat, cold raindrops. "Seems to be picking up speed. We better get moving."

"You're the boss, Tessy."

She waited for another slice of lightning to get her bearings, then began trudging forward again, keeping her ear turned to Jeremiah's progress behind her. *You're the boss, Tessy,* he'd said, and she reveled in his confidence. Yet at the same time, she inwardly admitted she'd rather follow. Still, she liked helping Jeremiah. She wouldn't mind always being his helpmeet.

Up ahead, strange, floating flashes of orange and yellow pierced the darkness. Tessy stopped, and Jeremiah stumbled to a halt beside her. She grabbed his arm. "Are—are those spirits?"

"No, not spirits. People…with torches."

His eyes were wide as he stared at the approaching flames, his jaw clenched. His entire body quivered.

She grabbed his arm. "What's wrong?"

"The fire glow at night." He gulped. "It brings back bad memories."

"From the war?"

"Yes."

She squeezed his arm. "War's over, Jeremiah."

"I know." Lightning sliced the sky, followed by a mighty thunder crash. "But it'll never be over for me, not until I can make things right over there." He gave her a tender, filled-with-regret look. "And here."

Another bright flash of lightning preceded thunder loud enough to raise the fine hairs on the back of her neck. "We can talk later. If those're torches up ahead, then people are lookin' for us. Doc send 'em out, you reckon?"

"Probably." Jeremiah heaved a sigh. "They'll wonder why we're together."

Tessy remembered the hurled accusation about dallying. She cringed. "Won't look good, will it?"

He raised one shoulder in a shrug. "All we can do is tell the truth. It's up to them to believe it or not."

Tessy inched forward, her hand still wrapped around Jeremiah's forearm. "You reckon they'll believe us about Ol' Gordy? Most folks didn't even know he lived out there."

"We'll make them believe, Tessy."

The fervency in his tone raised hope in Tessy's heart. Together they could convince the town. Together they could do most anything.

The weaving orange glow came closer, dividing into separate balls clearly distinguishable now as individual torches. And above the raging wind, voices called.

"Preacher? Hey, Preacher!"

"Jeremiah... Jeremi-i-i-i-ah!"

He cupped his mouth. "I'm here! Holden, I'm here!"

Tessy and Jeremiah moved in the direction of the torches while Jeremiah continued to call, until they met up with the six searchers. Holden handed his torch to Colt Murphy and embraced Jeremiah.

"Thank God you're okay. Callie and I were worried sick when you didn't come back." His gaze turned to Tessy, and his brows rose. "Tessy, I didn't expect to find you out here. Were you searching for him, too?"

The men angled stern gazes in Tessy's direction. She swallowed. If she said yes, no one could accuse her and Jeremiah of wrong-doing. But she couldn't bring herself to lie.

Jeremiah spoke over the roar of the wind.

"I saw Tessy heading out of town this morning, so I followed her."

All gazes turned to Jeremiah. The expressions, lit by dancing torch glow, held harsh shadows and forbidding lines.

"And I'm glad I did. We solved the mystery of the thefts, and—"

Colt Murphy cut in. "Preacher, I'm glad you're safe an' well, but standin' out here talkin' isn't the best idea. We need to get out of this storm." The wind whipped their clothing. The flames writhed at the end of the torches.

"We can talk tomorrow. Let's go."

Colt stepped to the front of the crowd and led the way. Holden braced Jeremiah's arm with his elbow, and Tessy fell into step beside the two men. Now that she and Jeremiah weren't alone and she wasn't responsible for leading him, her strength faltered. Her feet dragged the remaining distance to Shyler's Point.

The group separated at the edge of the town, the men heading to their own homes. Colt, Holden, and Jeremiah walked Tessy to her dogtrot. At the edge of the yard, Colt whirled on Tessy.

"Don't know why you're out here in this mess, but we'll take the time to sort it out tomorrow. Make sure you're here when I come by to talk."

"Yes, sir." Tessy's gaze drifted to Jeremiah. He looked ready to tumble off his crutch. She followed her impulse and placed a quick kiss on his cheek. "Thank you for your help today. I wouldn't've made it on my own."

He clasped her hand briefly. "You were as much help to me as I was to you. We'll talk again tomorrow." Then he chuckled. "Or, rather, later today. After church?" His chest tightened as words from his planned sermon tiptoed through his mind.

Tessy offered a small smile and nod.

Colt shook his head. "Ain't gonna be a church service. Already made the announcement to cancel. You won't be preachin' a sermon today, Preacher."

23

Jeremiah sank into the tubful of warm water, rested his elbows on the edge of the rolled tin, and released a deep sigh. Bless Callie for having the reservoir and pots of hot water ready for him. His stiff muscles slowly relaxed, and he wished he could stay in the steaming water for hours. But too soon the water turned tepid. Gooseflesh rose on his arms. He considered asking for more hot water, but it was nearly three in the morning.

He clung to the tub's slippery edge with one hand and grasped a rough towel with the other. His legs quivered with the effort of holding himself erect as he rubbed the towel over his body. He sat on the cold linoleum floor and wrestled his damp limbs into his pajamas. Finally, he called for Holden.

Holden dragged the tub to the lean-to while Jeremiah strapped on his braces. Holden returned and held out his hand. "Feel better?"

"Much better, thanks." Jeremiah allowed the other man to pull him to his feet. He perched on a kitchen chair and rested his chin in his hands. "Is Callie asleep?"

Holden poured two cups of coffee. He gave Jeremiah one and a deep draw from the other. "Yes. Since Evangelina's birth, she hasn't gotten a full night's sleep, but I think tonight was the longest she'd stayed up."

Guilt pricked. "I'm sorry I worried you two."

Holden shrugged, a grin climbing one cheek. "That's what friends are for."

Jeremiah reached across the table and clasped Holden's forearm for a moment. "You're good friends. Thank you." He released a long sigh. "It's been quite a night."

Raindrops pattered on the roof and dribbled down the foggy windows. The fury of the storm had already blown over, leaving behind a clean scent and the melody of gentle rainfall.

Holden took another sip of coffee. "After quite a day, I suppose."

Jeremiah nodded. "Tessy and I found the thief. An old man named Gordy who lived in a valley a few miles north of here. He said the town was to blame for his mother's death and for Tessy's unhappiness. So he stole to make the people pay."

Holden leaned forward. "Will he admit it to the sheriff so Tessy can be cleared?"

Sadness pressed against Jeremiah's chest. "He died

while Tessy and I were with him. We buried him on his property." He blew out a breath. "But we found all kinds of things hidden around his cabin. I could take Colt there in the morning and show him."

Holden shook his head. "After a storm like the one tonight, there will be limbs down, and the ground is slippery. Colt won't want to go—at least not for awhile."

Jeremiah wanted to settle this situation immediately. Then he remembered something. "Why were church services canceled? Was it because I was lost, or is it because the town is against me stepping behind the pulpit?"

"The storm. We never know how severe the mountain storms will be. Church was cancelled as a precaution so the hill people wouldn't come down in unsafe conditions." Holden grimaced. "To be honest, I don't know if folks would stay away if you were preaching. These people can be stubborn, and once they get their minds set on something, it's pretty hard to sway them."

Jeremiah believe him. For years the town had held to the stubborn belief that Tessy was responsible for every bad thing to befall the community. The sermon weighing his heart needed to be shared, and the sooner he had the opportunity to deliver it, the better he would feel.

A yawn pressed at his throat, and he gave way, allowing it to contort his face.

Holden smiled. "Jeremiah, go to bed." He yawned, too. "I'm ready for sleep. We can sleep late, then talk tomorrow after breakfast."

"I won't argue." Jeremiah rose stiffly and placed his crutch beneath his arm. "Whew, I worked muscles tonight I didn't know I had."

"That was quite a trek you took." Approval colored Holden's tone.

"It was worth it. Now I know for sure Tessy isn't a thief, and the town will know it, too. Next I'll let them know she isn't a jinx. Things will be different around here for her after that."

Tapping roused Tessy from a sound sleep. She rolled over, frowning. "Who is it?"

The door opened a crack and Mama's worried face appeared. "Colt is here and wants to see you. Get dressed and come out." She closed the door, apparently assuming Tessy would obey.

Tessy released a low groan and yanked the quilt over her head. Facing Colt first thing in the morning wasn't a good way to start her day. She'd fallen asleep thinking of Jeremiah and planning what she would say when she saw him. But now those words slipped away, replaced with the anxiety of finding the right words to tell Colt what she and Jeremiah had discovered about Ol' Gordy.

Throwing back the covers, she scooted out of bed. She

donned a clean dress from the hooks on the wall and ran a brush through her hair. Her hands quivered, making it difficult to control the brush. She wished she could sneak out the back door instead of facing Colt. Hopefully the conversation would be short.

She entered the main room. Mama was stirring a pot on the stove, and Colt was pacing back and forth. At her entrance, Colt spun and pointed a finger to the table. Tessy sat. He placed himself across from her.

"Thought you'd been told to stay home 'til we got this thievin' mess straightened out." Colt's glower sent chills through her. "Yet last night, there you were, runnin' loose."

Tessy swallowed and squirmed in her chair, feeling as welcome as a stray dog roving in trash bins. "I wanted to see a friend. Didn't expect to be gone so long, but…" Sorrow welled. How could Ol' Gordy be gone? She blinked against tears. "When I got to my friend's cabin, I found him real sick. While I was there…he died."

Mama released a gasp. She hurried to the table and placed her hands on Tessy's shoulders.

Colt's gaze narrowed. "That don't explain why you were out so late or why the city preacher was with you."

Still tired, Tessy tried to organize her thoughts. "Jeremiah—the preacher—followed me when I slipped out of town. I didn't know it 'til he was at the cabin. But I'm glad he was there, 'cause he said some words over Ol' Gordy and helped bury him."

Colt shook his head, as if trying to dislodge a burr from his ear. "You and the preacher dug a hole, plunked a man into it, and covered him up without filin' a death claim?"

Tessy cringed. She would give more care to burying to a dead raccoon than how the sheriff described Ol' Gordy's burial. "Preacher prayed over him. It was a simple service, but lovely. Ol' Gordy would've approved it."

Colt leaned back, his brow furrowed. "Ol' Gordy... You mean that scroungy half-breed hermit who lives in the valley? He was your *friend*?"

Tessy prickled. Colt shouldn't speak of Ol' Gordy that way. "Yes. Best friend I had 'til Preacher came along." Mama gave her shoulder an approving squeeze.

Colt smirked, and Tessy wished she could kick him a good one under the table. Then he swiped a hand across his chin, removing the grin. "So you visited this *friend*, buried him, and then what?"

"We gathered up all the stuff that'd been taken from town. We were gonna tote it back, but there was too much."

Colt raised a hand. "Whoa. You stashed your stolen goods at the cabin?"

"No. Jeremiah tried to tell you last night. Ol' Gordy took all that stuff."

Mama's hands convulsed on Tessy's shoulder, and

Tessy clasped one. "Before he died, Ol' Gordy confessed to stealin' things from people in town. Folks hadn't been helpful to him an' his ma, and he said they were mean to me, too. He wanted to make 'em pay, so he stole from 'em."

Colt's brows pulled so low his eyes became slits. "Are you blamin' some crazy ol' hermit for all the stealin' that's been goin' on around here?"

Tessy's chin quivered. "Yes."

Colt looped an elbow over the chair back. "I gotta tell you, this all sounds mighty convenient. How do I know you didn't hide stuff in the cabin of your ol' friend and then decide to blame it on him 'cause he's dead and can't defend himself?"

Tessy's face heated. Mama stomped out of the room. Tessy clenched her fists and met Colt's knowing leer. "'Cause my parents raised me to not tell lies or take things that aren't mine. Jeremiah was there. Ask him what Ol' Gordy said."

Colt poked out his lower lip. "I'll ask. But I don't put much stock in his word."

Tessy reared back, her jaw dropping. "Not put much stock—?" She shook her head. "How can you not put stock in the word of a minister?"

The sheriff barked a laugh. "He's a man, isn't he? A man who's fallen under your spell. He'd believe anything you told him. So it really isn't his word. It's yours."

"And my daughter's word is good enough."

Tessy swung around on her chair. Mama and Pop entered the room, Pop leaning on Mama's arm. His gray hair stood on end and his nightshirt sagged, but his eyes snapped with indignation.

"Colt, I've put up with all I'm goin' to concerning my daughter's supposed *ill wind*. Tessy's a good girl—an honest girl—and if she says the hermit took those things, then that's all that needs to be said. Verify it with Jeremiah Hatcher if you think you need to. Go out and dig that poor old man up if you have to. But as far as we're concerned, we're done with it."

Colt rose slowly, his frown aimed at Pop. "The town might see it different."

Pop raised his chin. "Don't much care. How I see it is all that matters to me." A smile crept across his whiskery cheeks. "I'll let the town know my thoughts in my own good time. But 'til then, if all you're gonna do is pester my daughter with accusations, I'd prefer you didn't come around here."

Colt stared at Pop with his jaw hanging. Then he snapped it shut and his expression turned hard. "I guess I'll go."

Tessy's gaze swung back and forth between the two men—stocky Colt and her frail-looking father. Yet somehow Pop appeared the stronger, the braver. Her heart pounded in love and pride.

Pop lurched forward one step, his hand extended. "Good-bye, Colt."

Colt clomped past Pop's hand, snatched his hat from a peg near the door, slapped it over his hair, and stormed out.

Jeremiah explained the previous day's events honestly and respectfully even though the sheriff's sour expression and snide tone raised his ire. When he finished, Colt snorted.

"You an' the McCleary girl have your stories straight. 'Course, you had the whole day an' most of the night to get it all arranged."

Jeremiah's temper flared. He prayed silently for patience. "There was no need for us to conspire on a story. We're speaking the truth."

"Time'll tell, I s'pose." Colt scratched his chin. "In a couple days, when things've dried out, we'll head back down to that valley and snoop around. Until then, no traipsin', Preacher. And it'd be in your best interest to keep your distance from Tessy McCleary."

If Jeremiah had two sturdy legs he'd spring from this chair, wave a fist under the sheriff's sanctimonious nose, and tell him exactly what he thought of his unwarranted suppositions. "I've done nothing wrong, and neither has Tessy, so I won't accept being under house arrest." He struggled to his feet as Colt rose to tower over him. "I'm not trying to be disrespectful, but I stand innocent before my Highest Authority. In time, you'll see the truth, too."

Colt spun on a heel and headed for the door. He grabbed the door handle but then stopped and sent a smirking grin over his shoulder. Swinging the door wide, he gave a flamboyant wave of his hand. "Come right on in, Miss McCleary."

24

Tessy glanced at the passage leading to the dogtrot's bedrooms. Seemed hours had passed since Mama, Pop, and Jeremiah closed themselves away in Mama and Pop's bedroom. She'd washed the breakfast dishes, dried them, put them away. Scrubbed the table, added a checked cloth and a crockery bowl of pine cones. Swept the floor beneath the table, shook out the rug. And still they hadn't returned.

She tiptoed to the closed door, temptation teasing to go in and find out why Pop asked her to fetch Jeremiah. She raised her fist, ready to tap, and the door swung wide. She jumped back, not wanting to be caught hovering near like an eavesdropper. Mama came out first, a soft smile gracing her face. Jeremiah followed more slowly, leading with his crutch. The determined light in his eyes raised Tessy's curiosity another notch.

Jeremiah caught hold of Tessy's elbow. "May I have a

moment of your time?"

His voice held his southern twang, and Tessy's heart rolled over. She nodded.

He gestured to the front door. "Let's step outside, shall we?" Once outside, he lightly gripped her upper arms. "I won't be able to see you the rest of this week. I'm sorry, because I know we need to get some reading and writing lessons in, but I…" He bit down on the inside of his upper lip, his brow furrowing.

Her heart pounded and the blood rushed to her head. Why did this man create so many raging emotions? Shouldn't having a friend be easier? Knowing she'd be denied his company brought an unexpected ache.

He sighed. "This coming Sunday will be my last sermon here in Shyler's Point. Your pop is well enough to take over his duties again."

Tessy fought an urge to cry. Happiness for Pop's recovery battled with sadness at Jeremiah's certain departure. She hung her head.

"I was pretty upset when Colt told me he'd cancelled services for today. But after talking to your father, I'm glad for the rainstorm. I would've created a different kind of storm and made a mess of things by letting anger get the best of me. God gave me a chance to do things His way instead of mine. Much rests on my last sermon, Tessy. I want to be God's instrument, His voice. And that means I need time alone with Him in prayer and Bible study." He squeezed her arms. "I don't want you to think I'm staying away due to anything Colt said."

Slowly she raised her gaze. Jeremiah's face reflected earnestness to be heard and believed.

"What Colt said, about me being with you to watch you—"

Tessy stepped free of his touch. "It don't matter, Jeremiah."

"It does matter." He held her captive with the sincerity in his blue eyes. "Yes, at first I wanted to spend time with you to watch you, but not to prove you were a thief, only to prove you weren't."

She frowned.

"I thought if I watched you I could tell everyone I never saw you take something that didn't belong to you. I wasn't watching you because I didn't trust you, but because I did trust you and believed in your innocence. Do you understand?"

Some of the hurt melted away under his honest gaze. "Yes."

"There will probably be some who see me keeping my distance from you and find reasons to explain it away. But I'm not isolating myself away from you, I'm isolating myself with God." He paused, searching her face. "Do you believe me?"

If she believed him, and he proved untruthful, her heart would shatter. But she wanted to believe him. Despite all of the hurts bestowed by people in the past, all of the mistreatment and misunderstandings, she wanted to believe Jeremiah. Even if it meant being let down again.

"Tessy?"

She released a sigh. "I believe you."

The smile breaking across his face was the most beautiful thing Tessy had ever seen. Tears pressed behind her lids. Her simple words had more effect than she could ever have anticipated. Even if something happened— even if in the end he disappointed her somehow—seeing that moment of unbridled joy made the possible hurt worth it.

He took her hand, giving it a squeeze. "Take care, Tessy. I'll see you in a week." He released her hand and stumped away. Although his steps were slow, it seemed like a weight had been lifted from him.

Tessy sat on the front stoop and watched until he rounded the corner and disappeared from view. He'd spend this week in prayer—isolated with God, he'd said. Well, she would follow his example. She'd pray, too. If Jeremiah was only planning to be in Shyler's Point one more week, he'd need someplace to go. Far as she knew, God hadn't opened any doors to churches for him yet, so she'd pray for that. And she'd pray for herself, for her new start in Searcy.

The soggy ground pulled at Jeremiah's crutch, making the path difficult to navigate. The conversation with Reverend McCleary played in his mind, and eagerness to start on his Bible reading and prayer made him impatient with his slow process.

The air smelled different after last night's storm— earthy, yet clean. Would the plan he and the good reverend had concocted bring a fresh cleansing to the townspeople's spirits? Birds sang, their cheerful song a perfect accompaniment to the hope he held in his heart.

Shifting his gaze to the clear blue sky, he smiled. "I'm countin' on You to soften their hearts like last night's rain softened the ground. Let the message we're preparing pierce their darkness and leave a lasting light. You've got the power to heal, so heal the fear in this town."

For the next three days Jeremiah only emerged from his room for meals. Wednesday noon when he seated himself at the dinner table, Holden handed him an envelope. Jeremiah peeked at the return address. He frowned.

Callie placed a plate of ham and beans in front of him. "Not bad news, is it?"

Jeremiah ran his finger beneath the flap to open it. "Every time I see the word Poland, I'm reminded of how difficult things are for the Jews in that country right now."

Holden took his plate from Callie. "Jeremiah, I know you feel as if you failed while in Europe, but Callie and I view what you did as nothing short of miraculous."

Jeremiah lifted his gaze from the envelope. "Miraculous?"

"Yes. Because of you, lives were saved. Children are in homes with families who will care for them and give them the chance to grow up and become whatever this country allows them to be."

Callie placed her hands on Holden's shoulders. "That's right."

Jeremiah fought a lump in his throat. "But there were so many I couldn't save…" Familiar sadness struck again.

Holden shook his head. "You made a difference. God weeps with you for the lives that were lost, but do you think He holds you responsible? You worked on the side of right over there, and Callie and I are proud of you."

Callie nodded. "Be proud of yourself, Jeremiah. Give thanks for the lives you touched." She sat at the table. "Reverend McCleary once said that even if only one person was willing to accept the gift of salvation, Jesus would still have submitted to the cross. If you'd known in advance that you could only save one child from Hitler's rampage, would you have decided it wasn't worth the risk?"

Jeremiah reared back. "Of course not!"

Callie smiled. "You did so much more than save one

child. Be thankful. As Tessy so wisely told you, God looks on the motivation of a man's heart and judges his desire to do right, not only his finished works. If God willingly accepts what you gave, why do you refuse to see it?"

Tears clouded his vision, but Jeremiah couldn't hold back a smile. What wonderful friends these two were. God had put him in this place, with these people, to find his healing. "You're right, Callie. I need to praise God for each life He allowed to come out of Europe. He has a plan for those children, and I need to be thankful that His plan will find fulfillment through those lives."

"That's more like it!" With an impish grin, she pointed at the plates of food. "Cold beans are awful. So pray, will you?"

That evening Jeremiah stepped behind the pulpit with a heavy heart. Only a spattering of townsfolk had come. For a moment he considered canceling the Bible study, but Tessy's presence in her familiar front row seat changed his mind. Jesus would have died for one contrite sinner. Jeremiah would have risked his life to save only one Jewish child. So this evening he would share even if only one person took the lesson to heart.

He'd chosen Psalm 23, focusing on the reference to Jesus as the shepherd. The image was one of tender care and compassion. As he explained the duties of the shepherd to his flock, he relied on Tessy's attentive gaze to bolster him. The others seemed closed to the sweet words he'd hoped would soften their hearts. But Tessy—ah, Tessy—soaked up the words, giving him the courage to continue despite the disapproval emanating from most of the congregation.

When he finished his lesson, Holden led the hymn "Gentle Shepherd," a perfect ending to the evening. Still, the singing sounded flat. The song ended, and people rose, but Jeremiah held up his hand.

"Wait, please. I have an announcement."

The townsfolk paused, turning their impatient gazes in his direction.

He squared his shoulders and forced a smile. "This coming Sunday I will deliver my farewell sermon to your community. It's not a message for the weak at heart, but I believe it's a message God wants every member of Shyler's Point to hear."

A murmur went across the small crowd.

"I hope to see you Sunday."

Still mumbling, the people filed out. Tessy remained in her pew, her expressive gray eyes wide. Jeremiah hitched his way over and stopped several feet from her. Her sweet face lifted in a soft smile, and it took great control for him not to reach for her hand.

"I reckon you'll be speakin' to a packed room on Sunday after what you just said. Word'll get around that you said the weak of heart shouldn't come. Nobody'll want to be accused of being that, so they'll come out in droves."

Was she pleased or worried at the prospect? "That's what I'm counting on."

She hunched her shoulders. "I trust you know what you're doin.'"

"I do."

A brisk nod sent her hair swinging. "Figured as much. You aren't weak at heart, Jeremiah Hatcher, an' I admire you for it."

His heart tripped at her compliment.

"I've been praying for you this week, that you'd find your course off this mountain." Pain briefly creased her face, but then she smiled. "God's got big plans in store for you. I just know it."

Jeremiah's heart lurched. He wanted to fold her in his arms and place his lips against hers. He wanted to whisper, *I love you.* He wanted to hear her say she loved him. But selfishness drove those desires, so he stayed still and quiet.

Tessy stood, closed the distance between them, and offered her slim hand. He took it. Her hand fit so neatly in his. A sweet smile lit her eyes. "Case I don't make it through the crowd on Sunday, lemme tell you now... Your bein' here has been special to me. Your friendship's a gift I didn't ever expect to receive. I'll always remember the lessons you've taught me." She blinked several times. "You've made a difference in my life, Jeremiah. Thank you."

He'd made a difference in her life. One life. One precious, infinitely priceless life. His soul sang with the wonder of her words.

She removed her hand from his grasp, offered one more tear-glittering smile, then slipped out of the church.

Jeremiah sank onto a pew—at her spot—and replayed each word she'd spoken. Replayed his own heart-lifting response to her words.

Heavenly Father, I love Tessy. I love her more than I thought possible. But I love You more. You're making clear to me what I'm to do—where I'm to go. I don't yet know how You'll work it out, but I know You'll make it possible. Right now every part of me longs to ask Tessy to join in my work, to make her a part of the rest of my life. But I don't want to ask her out of selfishness. Give me a sign, God. You moistened the fleece for Gideon, so show me Your will in a way I can't misunderstand. And give me the courage to accept Your will, whatever it may be…

25

Sunday morning Tessy donned her best dress—yellow organdy with a crisp white collar. She smoothed her one pair of silk stockings over her legs, taking care not to catch the delicate fabric with her rough fingers. White shoes with a narrow buttoned strap and fairy-waisted heels completed the outfit.

She drew her hairbrush through her clean locks with long, slow strokes that sent tingles of pleasure down her spine. Or was the thought of seeing Jeremiah creating those delicious tingles? Her hair snapped and stood on end with electricity. Frowning, she rummaged in her drawer for the lace handkerchief Granny had given her on her sixteenth birthday. She tied it over her hair and then examined her appearance in the cracked mirror above her dresser. She couldn't compete with models in fashion magazines, but she'd do.

Walking to church between Mama and Pop while

an autumn sun beat down on their heads and a breeze teased their clothing was pure joy after Pop's long time in bed. He whistled a cheery tune. She'd wondered if it would be hard for him to witness someone else behind the pulpit, but she shouldn't have worried. His happiness at going gave her heart a lift.

How many Sundays had she made this journey across town with her parents? Melancholy panged as she realized her time here in Shyler's Point would come to a close soon with her move to Searcy, yet it was balanced with a sense of excitement. What might the future hold for her off of this mountain?

And what awaited Jeremiah? After today, he'd move on, too. Sadness nibbled at the edges of her heart. She'd miss him. He was her friend, and she loved him. But God had a plan for him, and it was best to let Jeremiah follow God's leading. Sorrow faded beneath a wave of joyous anticipation. What might happen for him next?

"Oh, my…" Mama paused, bringing Tessy and Pop to a halt with her.

The church yard overflowed with wagons and mules, automobiles, and milling town members. The Winters stood near the stairs talking quietly with Callie's aunts. Tessy scanned the yard, recognizing the Spencers, Ted Maness and his family, Colt Murphy… All of Shyler's Point must have turned out for this morning's service.

"Mama, Pop, I'm gonna run ahead and save us a spot."

Mama gave her a gentle nudge. "Yes, go ahead."

Tessy pushed through the crowd, dashed up the steps, and clattered into the sanctuary. She came to breathless halt in the middle of the aisle. Jeremiah stood in front of the simple altar that held an enormous, ages-old Bible. His head was bowed and his shoulders stooped. Praying. She held her breath and observed the white band of skin between his neatly cropped hair and the collar of his brown suit jacket. Her fingers itched to curve around those taut neck muscles and massage the tightness away.

Suddenly he turned and caught her staring. "Tessy…" He gaped at her, wonder blooming on his face.

How did he always make her feel so special? "Morning, Jeremiah." She poked her thumb over her shoulder. "Your words did the trick. Everybody's out there. Don't see how we'll all fit in the pews."

His eyes sparkled. "If Jesus could feed the multitude with a little boy's meager lunch, He'll find a way to stretch these benches to accommodate all of those waiting backsides."

Tessy laughed. She couldn't help it. Love welled up and spilled over. "Want me to open the doors an' let 'em know you're ready?"

"One minute, please." He buttoned his jacket, straightened his collar, then swung his crutch around and moved into position behind the pulpit. He stood tall, his chin high. "I'm ready."

Tessy's lips trembled. "My prayers are with you, Jeremiah Hatcher." She hurried to the doors and swung them wide.

People spilled in. So many mouths, yet no one spoke. They pressed tightly onto the benches, shoulders crunched, knees snug, children on laps. All gazes aimed to the front where Jeremiah stood, equally silent, an open Bible beneath his hands.

Mama and Pop entered last and joined Tessy at the end of the first pew on the left—her spot. The moment Pop lowered his frame to the spare inches of wooden bench, Jeremiah cleared his throat.

"Second Timothy, the first chapter, verses one through seven." He read straight through, but at the seventh verse, his reading slowed and he emphasized each word. "'For God hath not given us the spirit of fear; but of power, and of love, and of a sound mind.'"

His gaze swept across the room, and it seemed that no one even took a breath, so still was the waiting audience. "When Paul wrote this letter to Timothy, Christians were under attack, and Paul knew that he would be leaving his earthly life very soon. He wanted his beloved Timothy to understand how to persevere, how to toughen up and face the difficult moments that were waiting. He knew that when things are hard, it's easy to be afraid. So he reminded Timothy that fear does not come from God. God's spirit is one of power, of love—and a sound mind."

A breeze whisked in from the open doors and ruffled the pages of his Bible. He smoothed them tenderly. "When I came to this community just a few weeks ago, my heart was full of fear. I had come from war-ravaged Europe. I had lived with the sound of gunfire and the screams of dying. I'd witnessed families torn apart, cities destroyed. I'd tasted salty tears and sweat." Pain pinched his brow. "I'd crept through dark landscapes, my heart pounding in my ears, on missions to relieve the suffering of Jews forced into hiding." He shuddered, hunching forward as if receiving blows. "Fear was my constant companion."

He straightened, his expression grim. "I came here for healing. My first view of your beautifully majestic mountains made my soul hopeful that healing would come. The love shown to me by many of you"—his gaze bounced from the Winters to Callie's aunts to little Jimmy and lingered on Tessy—"helped soothe the wounds the war left on my heart. But as I came to know you, to become familiar with this community and its people, I came to realize something."

His brows lowered. "Fear resided here, too. Not fear of gunfire or bombs falling from the sky. Not fear of Hitler's henchman storming through town and carrying people away. But fear of a girl. A slip of a girl. A girl who, according to your beliefs, carried an ill wind that could bring harm to you."

A soft murmur swept across the room.

Jeremiah leaned forward. "But listen to the words from God. He doesn't give us a spirit of fear! His Spirit is power. Power to throw off the bonds of superstition that hold us captive. His Spirit is love. Love that looks beyond our external trappings to the person underneath. His Spirit is of a sound mind—one that recognizes the only real truths are the ones found within the pages of His Book."

Tessy's heart pounded with the surety in his tone, the compassion in his eyes. This was God's message.

"At the end of this second letter, Paul warns that people will turn their ears from the truth and will believe in fables." He lifted his Bible and held it high. Tears shone in his eyes, evidence of his fervent desire to break through the chains of fearful superstition and release God's love in this community. "Dear people, believe me when I tell you superstition is fable. Superstitious beliefs are lies designed by the evil one to harden your hearts and keep you from realizing God's perfect plan for each of you. That's why, in verses 14 through 17 of the third chapter, Paul admonishes Timothy—God admonishes us—to continue in the training we've received from His word."

The Bible's pages rustled in the breeze easing through the sanctuary, touching each person much the way the Holy Spirit touched each believer on the day of Pentecost.

"He reminds us to go to these scriptures to understand what is profitable for doctrine, for reproof, for correction, for instruction in righteousness, so that we may be furnished for good works." Slowly he lowered his hand, bringing the Bible to the podium. "For good works. Not evil."

Jeremiah bowed his head, as if gathering strength. When he raised his face again, tears streamed down his cheeks. "How man's evil has pained my heart. Hitler's attacks on the innocent... I'll never be able to erase those pictures from my mind." His voice sounded choked with repressed sobs. "Such pointless acts of cruelty. I wanted to escape that inhumanity. But here, on this mountain, surrounded by God's beauty, I found it again."

Tessy realized that her face was wet. She raised her hand to sweep away her tears, and at the same time Jeremiah wiped his palms across his cheeks.

"I found it in the loneliness of an old man who lived all by himself in a shadowed valley rather than face the contempt of those who lived on the sun-laden mountainside. I found it in the sorrow of a young woman ostracized and held to blame for events outside of her control." Deep grief contorted his face. "Here in the sunshine of God's beauty I found people living in a dark shadow, acting in fear instead of in love, inflicting harm instead of offering acceptance."

He shook his head, hope igniting on his face. "But

it doesn't have to be that way. We can live the way God wants us to live if we release our fears and allow His Spirit of power and love to bring us to a sound mind set on Him and His truth." He drew in a shuddering breath and placed his hand on his chest. "I'm not perfect. But God's mercy and grace have brought me here to find healing from fear and pain. God's mercy and grace can do the same thing for you, if only you'll let Him. Please reach out to Him."

He extended his hand, his open palm seeming to wait for someone to grasp hold. "Open your hearts and minds to His love. Adopt it for yourselves, and live together in harmony and peace rather than fear and accusation." His head dropped low, his hands curled around the edges of the pulpit, and his shoulders sagged.

Pop rose and strode across the floor. He laid his arm across Jeremiah's slumping shoulders. "This young man found the courage to speak the words I've held silent for over twenty years. I stand before you now to ask forgiveness. From my daughter, for never bringing to an end this season of mistreatment and pain. And to you, for allowing you to continue in your misguided beliefs in jinxes and curses and ill winds."

Pop turned his gaze on Jeremiah. "Preacher, you delivered God's message to us today. You've done your part. Now it's up to us to accept it or to continue in evil's way." He gave Jeremiah a clap on the shoulder and stepped forward, his fervent gaze sweeping across every face in the room. "Make your choice today. Second Timothy three, verse sixteen, '...from a child thou hast known the holy scriptures, which are able to make thee wise unto salvation through faith which is in Christ Jesus.' Will you stand up and proclaim that faith today?"

The floorboard creaked—Callie and Holden rising. From the other end of the pew, Vivian and Viola popped up side-by-side, hands clasped, fuzzy chins high and eyes glittering. Then little Jimmy Peterson and his mother, Nancy Kirby, Flossie Tate... One by one, across the room, people got to their feet.

Ted Maness jumped up, but he stalked to the open doors. He turned a derisive glare in Pop's direction before stomping down the steps.

Pop didn't cringe. He raised his hands. "Let's sing. 'What a friend we have in Jesus...'"

Voices joined in, but Tessy couldn't sing. The change that had just swept through the room left her giddy and light inside, yet something pressed against her voice box, stilling any sound. She listened, her chest tight, her heart pounding, thankfulness filling her chest. Then someone tapped her on the shoulder, and she turned. She sucked in a breath.

Pete leaned forward and spoke directly into her ear. "Step outside, Tessy." He turned, and she followed automatically. The hymn poured through the open window and surrounded them with its sweet message of hope. He led her to the side of the church where a man Tessy had never seen before waited in the shade of the building.

Pete ushered her to the man. "Tessy, this is Professor Warren, who is in charge of the botany department at the college. Professor Warren, my sister, Tessy."

Tessy shook the man's hand. "Hello, sir."

"So this is the young artist." Professor Warren beamed. "Has Pete given you the good news?"

Tessy gaped at the two men. What was going on?

"Not yet." Pete seemed to twitch with excitement. "Tessy, do you remember the drawing you sent me?"

She scowled, thinking. "You mean the beaver dam?"

"Yes. I showed the drawing to Professor Warren. He is in the process of writing a book detailing the flora and fauna of Arkansas."

She wrinkled her face.

"Plants and animals."

Tessy hunched her shoulders. "Oh."

"He's been searching for an artist to create the plates for his book, and he—"

The professor rubbed his palms together. "Young woman, I'd like to offer you the contract."

Tessy shook her head. "I don't understand."

Pete curled his hand on her shoulder. "If you make drawings for the book, you'll be paid for your work."

"Paid to draw?" They must be playing a joke.

"I assure you it will be a substantial amount." Professor Warren fixed her with a serious look. "Initially, you'll be paid for your time and your product. Then, when the book is published, you'll receive royalties."

"A portion of the monies earned," Pete said.

The professor chuckled. "Based on the popularity of such projects in the past, this could prove to be quite financially beneficial for you, young woman."

Substantial amount... Published book... Royalties... Financially beneficial... Tessy's head spun. She looked from one man to the other, at a loss for words.

"Well, Tessy, what do you say?" Pete waited, his gray eyes wide and hopeful. For the first time, Tessy read something other than disappointment in his gaze.

"I—"

"Tessy, may I speak to you?"

She turned at the quiet request. Jeremiah stood a few feet behind her. People spilled across the yard, and a group surrounded Pop and Mama. Suddenly all she wanted was to be alone with Jeremiah.

She touched her brother's coat sleeve. "I'm very interested in the project, and I wanna talk to you about it more. Will you come to the house for lunch? We can talk then. But right now I have to talk to Jeremiah."

26

Jeremiah led Tessy through the woods to the Little Muddy. On the way, he gathered a handful of wild-flowers the same yellow as her dress. She blushed sweetly when he gave them to her, and the bloom in her cheeks was more beautiful than any flower could ever be.

They settled side by side on the rock near the beaver's dam. The church service had taxed his emotions, but the majesty of the mountains filled him with an inner strength that surpassed human frailties.

A few strands of Tessy's honey hair pulled loose from the handkerchief tied around her head like a Russian *babushka*. The wisps lifted gently in the sweet smelling breeze. She'd never covered her hair that way before. The babushka was his fleece. He wanted to tell her about God's sign, wanted to ask for her hand. But should he propose marriage when he had so little to offer?

Tessy laid the bouquet on the rock between them and

picked up a deep auburn maple leaf. She tore the leaf into tiny pieces, flinging the bits one-by-one into the river. When she'd emptied her hand, she released a light laugh. "Did you wear out your talker this morning?"

He gave a start. "What?"

"You weren't short of things to say at the service, but now I can't coax a word out of you."

Jeremiah gave a self-deprecating chuckle. "I'm trying to find the right words."

She smoothed her skirt over her knees and peeked at him out of the corners of her eyes. "I like flowers growin' in a meadow or prettying up a vase, but I'm not one for flowery speeches, Jeremiah. You can speak plain."

He smiled. "I reckon I can do that."

"I know you can. 'Specially after what you did this morning." Bright tears glittered in her eyes. "What you did, makin' that whole town look at me and see something besides a dimwitted jinx…"

"Because you're not a dimwitted jinx. You are a child of God, created in His image, with gifts and abilities designed for His glory." His fervor grew, and all he felt for her demanded release. "The town and their fool notions tried to convince you otherwise, but I always knew it wasn't true. You're a beautiful person, inside and out, and I love you."

Tessy sucked in a breath of surprise. Jeremiah's heart clutched, and even the squirrels ceased their chatter for a few incredulous seconds. Her gray eyes spilled their tears, yet joy lit her face.

"You—you love me, Jeremiah?" The query emerged in a breathy, wavering whisper.

Jeremiah captured her hands. "Yes, I do. Very much."

"You love me…" A slow smile lifted the corners of her lips and her fingers pressed into his palms. "Jeremiah Hatcher, the preacher man, loves me." Her shoulders straightened, her chin raised. Her bearing became queenlike.

Tears threatened as he witnessed the power his words had on her. Had no one ever said them to her in her lifetime?

She giggled, her face crinkling in delight. "Tell me why, Jeremiah. Tell me why you love me." She gazed at him intensely, as if trying to read the answer in his eyes.

He placed her palms against his chest and held them there so she could feel the thrum of his heartbeat. "I love you because you have a tender heart. I love you for the carefree way you move through the woods, so graceful and at ease. I love you for the way you listen and absorb the messages I share from the pulpit on Sundays—I see God's love shining in your eyes when I look out on the congregation. I love your hair, the way it lifts in the breeze and shines in the sun. I love your gray eyes that always seem to seek approval."

He slipped his arms around her and pulled her close.

"But you don't need to seek approval. You have it with God, and you have it with me. I love you, Tessy Mc-Cleary."

She pressed her cheek to his shoulder, her palms firm against his chest. "I love you, too, Jeremiah Hatcher."

Jeremiah shifted her away slightly then lowered his lips to hers. Her breath was warm and moist, her lips innocent as she offered herself to him. "Oh, Tessy…" He pulled the handkerchief from her hair and ran his fingers through the silky strands. His heart rejoiced that this woman—this special, beautiful, compassionate woman—loved him. She truly loved a crippled, down-hearted minister.

She grazed his jaw with her fingertips. "Jeremiah?"

"Yes, dear one?"

"I've never been so happy in all my life."

Tears stung. "I know. I know, Tessy."

They held each other as the music of the woods—the birdsong, the wind's whisper, the stream's gurgle—filled their ears.

After long, wonderful minutes, Tessy sighed. "What do we do now?"

Jeremiah wove his fingers through hers. "We're to marry. I know it's what God intends. But beyond that? I don't know. I believe God is calling me back to Europe to minister to the displaced Jews, but He hasn't given me the means to get there."

She sat up, her gray eyes flying wide and joy igniting on her face. "I do."

Jeremiah frowned. "You do…what?"

She laughed and threw her arms around his neck, nearly toppling him from the rock. "I have the money!"

He disengaged himself from her stranglehold. "What are you talking about?"

"That man in the churchyard—the man with Pete?" Her words tripped over each another like the creek over stones. "He's a professor of plants and animals, and he saw one of my drawings—I sent one to Pete when I was mad at you and wanted to get even—and he's writing a book, and he said he'd pay me to draw the plates for it, and— Oh! Jeremiah! We can do it!"

She leaped up and twirled a happy circle. "There will be royalties, so we can do it! Don't you see?"

Jeremiah didn't understand, but he enjoyed her exuberance too much to squelch it.

She plunked down next to him and rested her cheek on his shoulder. She toyed with the flowers. "Of course, we won't be able to leave immediately. I have to do lots of drawings first, but he might be able to use some from my drawing pad. And I want a real wedding, Jeremiah, with Callie for my bridesmaid, and a cake, and a gown. Mama can make it. I want to meet your family, all of them, before we get aboard that big ship and go across the ocean." She tipped her head to peer at him. "Is that okay?"

Joy danced in his soul. "I want all of those things, too. I can't wait for my mama and daddy to meet you. They'll love you as much as I do."

"Oh, I hope so." She sat quietly, her head on his shoulder, her hair tickling his cheek. After awhile she giggled again.

"What's funny?"

"Us." She sat up and placed her palms on the flat rock next to his thigh, smiling into his eyes. "Who would've guessed God would match up a minister with a—"

Jeremiah silenced her with one gentle finger against her lips. He would never allow that word to be spoken again. Not by anybody. "With the most beautiful woman in the world."

Her eyes filled. "Oh, Jeremiah…"

He pulled her close, and when they met in a kiss, the sweetness was beyond anything he could have imagined.

Acknowledgments

I first must thank my readers who wanted to read Jeremiah's story. I hope you will find his "happily-ever-after" satisfactory.

Of course thanks to my family, who put up with me tap-tapping far into the night, serving store-bought dinners, and talking about imaginary people as if they're real. Your support is a real blessing.

Thank you to my parents, who always encouraged me to write and who are my most exuberant cheerleaders. I'm so grateful that of all the parents in the world, God gave me you.

To my wonderful posse members who make me laugh, who pray for me and keep me grounded. You are definitely a blessing in my life.

Finally, and most importantly, praise be to God who makes wonderful plans for us and sees those plans to completion. When we think things are falling apart, they are so often simply falling into place. Thank You for all You are to me. May any praise or glory be reflected back to You.

Est. 2013

Wings of Hope Publishing is committed to providing quality Christian reading material in both the fiction and non-fiction markets.

CPSIA information can be obtained
at www.ICGtesting.com
Printed in the USA
LVOW04s1502090117
520295LV00001B/72/P